W9-AEC-491

DESTINATION: LOOP

From the publishers of the Shortline RR Series

Straw hat time in Chicago. It's July 1, 1925, and most of the passengers crowding the Adams and Wabash station on the Union Loop appear more interested in the photographer than in watching the arrival of their Chicago Rapid Transit train. (George Krambles Collection)

Brian J. Cudahy

DESTINATION: LOOP

The Story of Rapid Transit Railroading In and Around Chicago

Brattleboro, Vermont
Lexington, Massachusetts
THE STEPHEN GREENE PRESS

A WORD OF THANKS

MORE PEOPLE than can possibly be mentioned deserve thanks and appreciation for their assistance in the preparation of this book. First mention clearly must go to George Krambles, recently retired from the position of Executive Director of the Chicago Transit Authority. Krambles not only supplied many of the period photographs* that appear in the following pages, but he continually took time to explain many facets of rapid transit in Chicago with a clarity that few can match. Harold Geissenheimer, CTA's current General Operations Manager, was also most helpful in supplying contemporary data and information. A special note of appreciation is due the Chicago Historical Society. CHS supplied several important photographs* for the book, and also published a significant portion of Part One in the CHS magazine, *Chicago History*. B.G. Cunningham, of the Regional Transportation Authority, was always willing, to track down some elusive fact or other, and Thomas Meagher, president of Continental Air Transport, was helpful in providing information on his company's predecessor firm, the Parmelee Transportation Company.

And finally: in Chapter Five we read of Frank Hedley, a transit executive who began his career on the elevated lines of Chicago, and who in later years became the General Manager of the Interborough Rapid Transit Company in New York. This book is dedicated to the memory of a man whose career was the reverse of Hedley's, who began work on the subways of New York in 1932, who rose to major executive positions with both the Board of Transportation and the Transit Authority in New York, and whose final post was that of Chief Operating Officer of the Regional Transportation Authority in Chicago. Leo Cusick died in the Spring of 1982, but during 1975 and 1976, in the early and hectic days of the RTA, he and the author spent many evenings together trying to understand the dynamics of mass transit in the nation's second largest city. May he rest in peace.

Burke, Virginia. July, 1982

**Unless otherwise credited, all photographs are by the author.*

This book is manufactured in the United States of America. It is designed by R. Dike Hamilton and published by The Stephen Greene Press, Fessenden Road, Brattleboro, Vermont 05301.

Library of Congress Cataloging in Publication Data

Cudahy, Brian J.
Destination loop.

Includes bibliographical references and index.

1. Chicago (Ill.)—Transit systems—History.
2. Chicago Metropolitan Area (Ill.)—Transit systems—History. I. Title.
HE4491.C48C83 1982 388.4'4'0977311
82–11953
ISBN 0–8289–0480–4

Chronology

1833 Village of Chicago established

1837 City of Chicago incorporated

1848 First passenger train reaches Chicago over Galena & Chicago Union Railroad. Chicago River "reversed"

1856 First Illinois Central suburban train operates between Chicago and Hyde Park

1859 First Chicago horse-drawn street railway

1863 World's first subway opens in London

1869 First proposal to build an L in Chicago

1871 Michigan Central & Rock Island Depot opens. Great Chicago Fire

1880 Chicago & North Western Railway Depot opens. Original Union Station opens

1883 Adams Law enacted. First Chicago cable cars operate on State Street

1888 First successful streetcar electrification in Richmond, Virginia

1892 South Side L opens for business

1893 First Chicago streetcars electrified; Lake Street L opens

1894 Yerkes purchases Lake Street L and obtains franchise for Northwestern L

1894-96 Yerkes gets franchises for Union Loop

1895 Metropolitan West Side L opens

1897 First American subway opens in Boston. Union Loop L service begins. Sprague perfects m.u. control

1900 Northwestern L opens

1902 Chicago voters opt for publicly operated transit. First Chicago subway proposal from Bion Arnold

1906 All Chicago streetcars electrified

1907 Ordinances renewing street railway franchises also establish a fund for future subway construction

1911 Current Chicago & North Western Depot opens

1913 Through-routing begins on Ls. Fifth Avenue becomes Wells Street south of Chi-

CONTENTS

cago River in April, reverts to Fifth Avenue in July

1916 Fifth Avenue becomes Wells Street south of Chicago River

1919 North Shore interurbans operate on Loop

1924 Chicago Ls merge to form Chicago Rapid Transit (CRT)

1925 Skokie Valley line opens on the C,NS&M

1926 Illinois Central RR's suburban service electrified; South Shore interurbans reach downtown Chicago

1932 CRT and Insull's Middle West Utilities enter receivership. Insull indicted

1934 Insull returned to America and acquitted

1937 Chicago applies for federal aid to build subways

1938 Ground broken for State Street subway

1941 "Electroliners" delivered to North Shore

1943 State Street subway opens

1945 Public referendum authorizes public transit authority in and around Chicago

1947 Chicago Transit Authority (CTA) takes over CRT and CSL. First of four experimental L cars delivered

1948 First 6000 series cars ordered. First Budd-built gallery car operates on CB&Q.

1951 Dearborn Street subway opens

1957 Chicago, Aurora & Elgin abandons passenger service

1958 CTA Congress line opens

1963 North Shore abandons all service

1964 Federal transit assistance program begins; CTA begins service on the Skokie Swift

1969 CTA Dan Ryan line opens. Old Tower 18 replaced by new structure

1970 CTA Kennedy line opens. Chicago Urban Transit District (CUTD) formed

1974 Creation of Regional Transportation Authority (RTA) approved by referendum

1982 First new interurban car since Insull era delivered to the South Shore line

AN INTRODUCTION TO

Chicago

(CHIEFLY FOR THOSE WHO HAVE NEVER BEEN THERE)

FAR OFF AND LONG AGO in the wilderness a small river gently emptied into Lake Michigan at a spot some thirty miles up the Western Shore from the lake's southern tip. Here, in 1803, twenty-seventh year of American independence and the second year of Mr. Jefferson's presidency, the United States army built a garrison, naming it Fort Dearborn for the incumbent Secretary of War. Surrounded by the vastness of the Northwest Territory, in a section soon to be designated the Illinois Territory, Fort Dearborn achieved historical prominence in 1812 as the scene of ignominious surrender and massacre. It was rebuilt in time to witness Illinois' entry into the Union as the nation's twenty-first state (1818) and the settlement of the immediate area until, in 1833, a village was established there and named "Chicago."[1] Population, three hundred fifty.

The community which was to become the nation's second largest metropolis achieved city status, courtesy of the Illinois legislature, in 1837, the year following Fort Dearborn's decommissioning, and conjunctively with the accession to the throne of England of a teen-ager named Victoria. When Her Britannic Majesty's reign concluded with her demise in 1901, Chicago numbered one and a half million population, and throbbed and bustled as a Midwestern center of business, industry and transportation—the railroad capital of America, in fact.

Meanwhile, what of the placid little river that quietly emptied into Lake Michigan? In 1848 the "can do"[2] burghers of Chicago decided that Nature had made a mistake. They reversed the current, turning it around so that since then the waters of Lake Michigan have flowed *into* the Chicago River and, with the cooperation of other waterways, both natural and man-made, on into the mighty Mississippi.

What couldn't be turned around—not that anyone wanted to—was Chicago's surging growth; not even the devastating fire of 1871 could check its expansion from five thousand population in 1840 to a million by 1890, still another million, almost, in a decade, eventually to top three million.[3] It was during the burgeoning years that William Vaughn Moody (1869–1910) would write: "Gigantic, willful, young, Chicago sitteth at the northwest gates . . . moulding her mighty fates."

The heartland of the city developed into a grid of avenues and streets extending some eight blocks east-to-west by ten blocks north-to-south, fronting on Lake Michigan and bounded on the west and north by the Chicago River. State Street is the dividing line between east and west sides; Madison Street demarcates the north and south sides. The intersection of these two thoroughfares is the epicenter from which all Chicago street numbering originates. In other cities such an area would be called "downtown," "center city," or suchlike term; in Chicago it is "the Loop."

Herein are clustered divers business-purpose buildings. LaSalle Street has emerged as Chicago's "Wall Street"; State Street is noted for its shops and Randolph Street for its theaters, not to mention Loop hotels and restaurants of national reputation and corporate headquarters of international influence. City

Hall is two blocks almost due north of the Loop's geometrical center. The Federal Building, Daley Center, the renowned Art Institute, and the Sears Tower are Loop landmarks. Just over the river at the Loop's northwest corner is the Merchandise Mart. Two avenue blocks from Michigan Avenue, easternmost street of the Loop, is the lake front.

So compact an area as the Loop was bound to become congested as the city grew and grew, eventually to 220 square miles extent, within a metropolitan area of 465 square miles. Mass transit was effected by a street railway network, itself expanding, featuring horse car and cable car accomodation, although some four-wheel electric trolley cars came on the scene in 1890. These surface lines terminated at or in the Loop, which got its name in the '80s because of the cable car routings therein. This explanation of the origin of "the Loop" is the conclusion of the Chicago Historical Society, searcher out and custodian of Chicago's past in fact and folklore.

Certainly there was no such thing as *rapid* transit in Chicago until 1892, when our story begins. Yet in less than a decade elevated rapid transit lines were in operation right where they are now, so that, as described by the Columbia Encyclopedia, "The elevated lines come into the heart of the city to make a huge rectangle for convenience in transfer. This is the celebrated Loop, which gives its name to the downtown section." The tourist guide books concur in this view.

After 1900 the horse cars and cable cars hung on vestigially, but faded away during 1906. One dares submit that in any word-association exercise on the subject of Chicago the response to "mass transit" would be "the Loop" or the "L." More generations of Chicagoans have lived "beneath the curved steel of the El, beneath the endless ties" than with the cable cars. Facts aside, most people today think downtown Chicago is called "the Loop" because of the L.

This book is perforce less about the Loop as a district than the Loop as an elevated railway. In referring to either aspect, we will always write it with the initial letter capitalized: Loop. The context should make clear which is meant.

Note that in the quotation above, from *The Neon Wilderness* by Nelson Algren, it says "El" to mean "elevated rapid transit railroad." We trust that this usage can be ascribed to a publisher's editor in New York or some other east coast city; in Chicago the same expression is routinely rendered "L."

Time now to turn the clock back to June 6, 1892, when rapid transit came to Chicago . . . .

Notes to Introduction

[1] A history of the city prepared by the Chicago Department of Public Works states that the name means "strong" or "great." Others say that it is an Indian word for "land of wild onions."

[2] Chicago today has a slogan: "Can Do. The Spirit of Chicago."

[3] In 1960: 3,550,404; metropolitan area, over 6,000,000. In 1980: 3,005,072; metropolitan area, over 7,000,000.

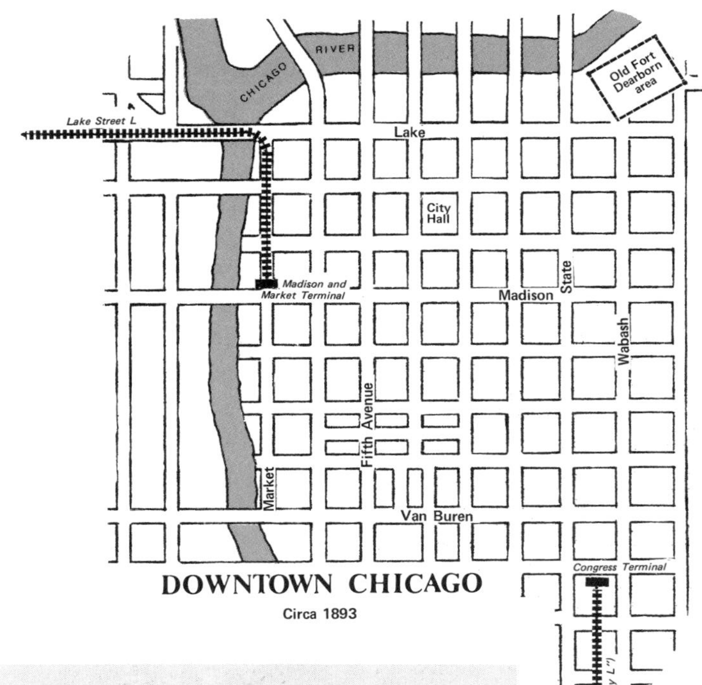

Above: Where's everybody going? It's October 9, 1893, and the World's Columbian Exposition is on the verge of closing its doors for good. But local residents have been invited to tour the fairgrounds on "Chicago Day." Many have undoubtedly gone to the exposition site riding the new South Side Rapid Transit elevated railway; others have crowded aboard surface cars—including resourceful types who have managed to convert trams which the builders thought were single-deck cars into double deckers. (Author's collection)

Opposite page: Intersection of the elevated tracks at Lake Street and Fift Avenue (now Wells Street), June 1900, less than three years after the ope ing of the Union Loop. That's Tower 18 near the diamond and, if you loo close, you'll see the switch rodding by which the towermen manually route traffic. Sixty trains an hour was the service level initially proposed; it took skilled operator to keep the traffic moving. (Chicago Historical Society

PART ONE
The Union Loop

CHAPTER ONE
Chicago's First L

JUNE 6, 1892—AN ELECTION YEAR—so that the big talk in Chicago that Monday morning was not about elevated trains and rapid transit; it was politics, politics, politics. The more so because delegates from all over the country were in Chicago, between trains, on their way to the Republican National Convention in Minneapolis. There they would nominate incumbent Benjamin Harrison on the first ballot to run for a second term, but that was in the future. For the present, an event which took place only hours previously had electrified citizens and politicos alike, so that the big, ongoing story was the machinations of *—Blaine, Blaine/James G. Blaine/ the continental liar/from the state of Maine!*

This down-east maverick had suddenly resigned from the lofty office of Secretary of State in President Harrison's cabinet to mount his own try for the Republican presidential nomination. Blaine had sufficient political clout to seriously alarm the Republican "Stalwarts." Hardly surprising, then, that delegates could spend the all-day train ride from Chicago to the Twin Cities—aboard high-stepping trains of the Chicago, Milwaukee & St. Paul Railroad—talking about and arguing over the political realignments which might ensue from this sensational development.

Nevertheless, had any of the parlor-car riding Republican regulars sought relief from political news on June 6, 1892, one item of interest could be found on page one of the second section of the afternoon *Chicago Tribune*, fresh copies of which were available from the white-jacketed Pullman porters. For that morning at precisely 7:00 o'clock the very first train on Chicago's first elevated rapid transit railroad commenced revenue service. Except for the Blaine presidential bid, the story surely would have been front-page news!

The line that opened in 1892 ran from a terminal south of Congress Street to 39th Street, a distance of 3.6 miles. The first revenue train was comprised of four wooden coaches hauled by a diminutive steam locomotive, which departed 39th Street with twenty-seven men and three women aboard. It took fourteen minutes to travel the length of the line. Actually, full schedules had been in effect since 5:00 A.M. to allow a final two hours of shakedown before the general public streamed aboard. The first five-cent fare on the line was paid by fourteen-year-old Freddie Cann, who lived at 4029 South Wabash Avenue. His ticket was collected by a company official, Supertendant Wetmore, resplendent in his spanking-new blue serge uniform with "S.S.R.T."—for South Side Rapid Transit—

embroidered on the collar in elegant gold thread. The full, resounding, official name of the line was "Chicago & South Side Rapid Transit Railroad Company."

A reporter for the *Chicago Tribune* noted that on the inaugural trip some passengers were part of "the lunch pail crowd," while others were described as "resembling gentlemen." The same scribe also expressed wonder that "entire strangers to one another freely discussed the novel journey." Two minutes after arriving at the Congress Terminal the train left, at 7:16, as the line's first southbound revenue trip.

There was no oratory or ribbon-cutting ceremony to mark the opening of the South Side line, although there had been some special trains operated for invited guests during the days immediately before the formal opening. Journalists commented that passengers who gazed out the windows as the L trains moved along at second story level "saw bits of domestic life usually hidden from the gaze of passing crowds," and also noted that "servant girls and chambermaids left their work to watch from back porches the fast-flying trains as they went by, and late breakfasts were probably explained on that score." The reference to "back porches" calls attention to what would soon become a unique feature of Chicago elevated lines in general, and the South Side in particular. Unlike the elevated lines in Manhattan and Brooklyn, New York (in 1892 these were the only other big city elevated railroad operations in the U.S.), where trains ran on structures built directly over public streets, Chicago made use of corridor-like alleys behind and between rows of buildings. The designation "Alley L" was long used as a popular name for the South Side route and, without the capital A, became a general synonym for any Chicago L so constructed. As will be seen shortly, Illinois state law governing the issuance of franchises for transit lines was responsible for the prevalence, in Chicago, of the alley routings.

The initial complement of equipment for the South Side L included twenty steam locomotives built in Philadelphia by the Baldwin Locomotive Works. Their design was, in general, in imitation of the highly successful engines developed for the New York City elevateds, providing storage for water and fuel in tanks behind and under the cab. The locomotives, having no tender, could operate in either direction without being turned. They were equipped with a very thoughtful accessory: a "full-length drip pan" to prevent grease, oil and scalding water from dropping to the ground below and landing on any Chicago citizen who happened to be in the way.

An order for passenger coaches was split between the Gilbert Car Company of Troy, New York, and the Wilmington, Delaware, firm of

Alley L construction. South of the Union Loop a Lake-Dan Ryan train heads for 95th Street over the former South Side Rapid Transit. Illinois law, in essence, caused the early L builders to prefer back-alley routes.

Jackson and Sharp. Each wooden car was forty-six feet long, weighed 42,500 pounds, and looked rather like a scaled-down version of a conventional open-platform railroad coach of the day. On the outside the cars wore liveries of glossy pale olive green, outlined with gold leaf trim and lettering. Interiors were done in natural oak and cherry.[1]

Operationally, the usual practice was to station two extra locomotives at the Congress Street station to serve as "relay engines." When a train braked to a halt at the northern terminal, the loco was cut off, and one of the relay engines coupled to the other end. Once the train left on its southbound trip, the inbound locomotive moved out to serve as relay power for a following train. Water and coal facilities were located south of 39th Street.

Most observers were happily impressed because the new line could traverse the route in half the time of the cable cars on State Street or Wabash Avenue, but a teacher in the Haven Public School at 15th Street was less than enthusiastic: "The noise and confusion in our schoolrooms are simply dreadful and distracting in the extreme," she exclaimed. Yet another negative appreciation was voiced by passengers who were accustomed to enjoying a smoke while traveling to work, a practice tolerated on the cable cars. Some potential passengers simply walked out of the new L stations when they realized that on-board smoking was prohibited; others tried to light up aboard the trains. One of the South Side conductors, when instructing his passengers on the regulations, would remind them that "this ain't no cable road."

However, the South Side did provide service around the clock, eliminating the anxiety of stay-out-late south siders over having to catch the "last car" on the cable railways, whose daily shutdown for inspection and maintenance of the cable and its associated apparatus effectively precluded twenty-four hour operation. During rush hours eighteen L trains were operated on a three-minute headway. After midnight trains ran every twenty minutes, two sets of equipment being sufficient for this service.

Inevitably, and promptly, the South Side would be compared with the New York elevated lines, the consensus being that the newer route "far surpassed Gotham's system in all respects." Such a conclusion was not surprising, for Chicago, at the wane of the century, was always comparing its local accomplishments with their New York City equivalents, and the conclusions were always the same. Thus did rapid transit make its modest beginnings on the shores of Lake Michigan.

Less than a year afterward, President Grover Cleveland—victor over Harrison in the November election—formally opened the World's Columbian Exposition in the Jackson Park section of Chicago, eight and one-half miles south of downtown. By this time twenty-six additional steam locomotives were in service on the South Side L, the car roster totaled 180 units, and service had been extended beyond 39th Street to the fairgrounds. Indeed, it was anticipation of the extraordinary traffic which the fair would generate, as much as any other single factor, that prompted construction of the South Side line in the first place.[2] Meanwhile, plans were already taking shape for more elevated lines in other sections of Chicago.

CHAPTER TWO
Chicago's Second L

IN CONTRAST to the sedately tranquil progress and businesslike opening of the South Side route, the story of the genesis and construction of Chicago's second L is a sordid one. More so than with any other Chicago L, the early days of the Lake Street line are associated with the bribe, the indictment, the kickback and the payoff; also hopelessly watered stock and various other unsavory things, among them a ludicrous boo-boo discovered at the very threshold of the line's November 1893 opening. The Chicago City Council had granted the line its franchise under the full legal panoply of a certain statute. Fine—except, it was discovered, that someone, somewhere in the course of events, had cited the *wrong* statute, thus throwing the status

In the days of steam power, the Lake Street L at Lake and Oakley. Loco No. 10 was built by Rhode Island, bore the name "Clarence A." Gilbert built open platform coach No. 7. Wonder of wonders, No. 10 has been preserved, and is on view in the National Museum of Transport, St. Louis. (George Krambles Collection)

of the about-to-open L into utter confusion. What the council had, in fact, authorized was not an elevated passenger railway, but an elevated coal-carrying conveyor belt!

The mistake turned out to be a clerical boner and was soon set right, whereas the line had other and more serious problems that were not so easily corrected. The franchise had been granted by the City Council in 1888. But its specifications were so restrictive that it had to be substantially revised in 1890. The original instrument would have lasted a mere twenty-five years, would have kept the line from crossing onto the east, or downtown, side of the Chicago River, would have required the use of virtually untested and certainly unproven technology,[3] and would have bound the franchise holder to lower the fare to four cents (i.e., twenty-five tickets for a dollar) after a period of two years. Such conditions made it very difficult to find willing investors to back the venture, and the 1890 revisions eased matters considerably. The later franchise provided for a term of forty years, for instance, thus allowing a longer period for the company to amortize its investment. Conventional rolling stock was also permitted.

The Lake Street franchise was held by one Michael C. McDonald, or "King Mike," as he was aptly nicknamed. McDonald had a checkered reputation; he was reputed to have garnered his early money via gambling and vice. Later, apparently, he was attracted to the less chancy field of

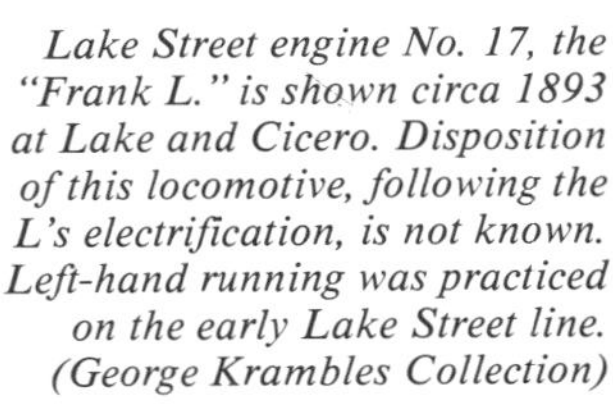
Lake Street engine No. 17, the "Frank L." is shown circa 1893 at Lake and Cicero. Disposition of this locomotive, following the L's electrification, is not known. Left-hand running was practiced on the early Lake Street line. (George Krambles Collection)

public transportation, in which he became a specialist. His forte was the organization of brand-new street railway companies—always in competition with existing lines—then selling out to the established operators at high prices. Unlike the bona fide businessman, for whom the securing of a franchise from the City Council was a difficult step, McDonald was able virtually to dictate to the aldermen—and therein was the key to his success. In association with a group of cronies McDonald was rumored to have control of twenty-three out of thirty-six votes in the City Council. Once having made considerable money on streetcar schemes, King Mike moved into the elevated railway business.

McDonald's aim with the Lake Street enterprise was less to build a functioning elevated line than it was to use his franchise to issue stock, then more stock, then still more stock, and to divert the proceeds of such sales to his own purposes. He and his "west side gambling fraternity" skimmed considerable profits from these multiple stock offerings, so that by 1892 the company's bonded debt stood at seventeen million dollars, whereas the actual value of its assets was less than four million.

McDonald and his crew began construction of the line but, because of the way they had plundered the project, they would never have been able to complete a structure and begin operations. Such, clearly, was not their intention. Thus in February of 1892 McDonald—who bore the title of treasurer in the company building the line—traveled to New York together with another Lake Street official, one Colonel M. H. Alberger. Supposedly they were about the business of furthering the construction of the Lake Street L. They put up at the Holland House, and while there McDonald granted an interview to *The New York Times.* He described the project in some detail and avowed that the purpose of this New York visit was to sell additional bonds in the Lake Street venture, and also purchase 16,000 tons of iron needed to finish the structure. But McDonald had planned otherwise; he felt that his time had come to exit the elevated railway business. Only a few days after the *Times* interview, it was announced that New York interests would purchase the entire Lake Street enterprise for slightly over two million dollars.

The elevated railways of Chicago will see a number of questionable deals and less-than-honorable characters over the years. But the reign of King Mike McDonald during the formative days of the Lake Street line is surely a high-water mark for out-and-out corruption of its kind.[4]

The new eastern owners infused fresh capital into the company and put the line in shape so that it was able to begin operations in November of 1893, a year and a half after the South Side opened. *The New York Times* gave the event a brief mention, but seemed more interested in the line's sordid past than its potential for improving Chicago's mass transit. Steam locomotives—thirty-five of them—were built by the Rhode Island Locomotive Works, and much resembled the design effected on the South Side's motive power. Rolling stock included 125 wooden coaches turned out by the Gilbert firm and Chicago's own Pullman Palace Car Company. As distinguished from an alley L, however, the Lake Street line's elevated structure was built directly over Lake Street, an important east–west thoroughfare. The line had its downtown terminal at Madison and Market streets; the latter of these is the present-day Wacker Drive. Proceeding north three blocks on Market, the route then turned west on Lake Street and ran almost six miles to Laramie Avenue.

With the inauguration of Lake Street service, an elevated line again demonstrated superior speed performance as compared to the older cable car operations. In mid-November a Chicago stockbroker went on record as follows: "I took an elevated train this morning and was landed at Market and Madison in fifteen minutes. If I had ridden on the cable, as has been my custom, it would have required thirty minutes." The rub was that the L's superior speed was useful only if one's destination was near the Market and Madison terminal at the periphery of the downtown business district. If one's place of work happened to be, say, at State and Adams, the plodding old cable cars could be far more convenient, and often faster, since they penetrated to the very center of the city.

Even with fresh capital and honest management the Lake Street line was not a sound operation. Its stock rose to twenty-eight dollars a share after McDonald sold out, but shrunk to eighteen dollars by July of 1894. The line would post an operating deficit of $146,000 during its first year of service. Also, in 1894, another new owner bought out the troubled line.

It was late in the preceeding decade that a Philadelphia syndicate with wide mass-transportation experience throughout the country had begun to buy up many of the surface car lines that crisscrossed Chicago. It is important to appreciate that throughout the 1880s and the 1890s the principal means of urban mobility in Chicago was the various horse car and cable car lines running along the city's streets. By most reckoning there were over thirty-five separate corporations engaged in such work in the early days of the horse cars. These were eventually merged into three major companies, one to the north, one to the west, and one to the south. It would be years, many years, before the fledgling elevated lines made any real dent in their business.

Seeing the Lake Street L as a potential threat to his West Chicago Street

Railroad, the point man for the Philadelphia syndicate—a broker by the name of Charles Tyson Yerkes, Jr.—negotiated the purchase of the company with an eye toward developing joint streetcar-rapid transit services in the west-side neighborhoods adjacent to Lake Street. Yerkes got the money-losing elevated line for the bargain price of a million dollars.

Yerkes was a clever and resourceful fellow. The son of a bank president, he was born in Philadelphia in 1837 and went to work as a brokerage clerk at the age of seventeen. At twenty-one he established his own brokerage firm; three years later he had his own bank. He was ruined in the Panic of

Charles Tyson Yerkes (1839-1905), chief promoter and builder of the Union Loop. (Chicago Historical Society)

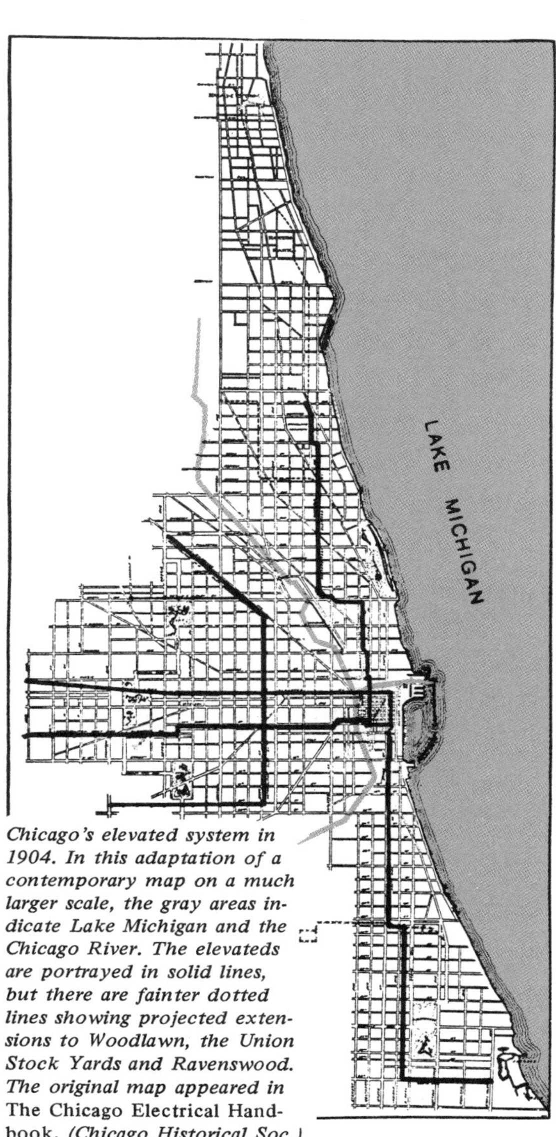

Chicago's elevated system in 1904. In this adaptation of a contemporary map on a much larger scale, the gray areas indicate Lake Michigan and the Chicago River. The elevateds are portrayed in solid lines, but there are fainter dotted lines showing projected extensions to Woodlawn, the Union Stock Yards and Ravenswood. The original map appeared in The Chicago Electrical Handbook. *(Chicago Historical Soc.)*

1871 and then imprisoned for failure to give "preference" to the City of Philadelphia over other creditors during the collapse. After seven months in jail he was pardoned by the governor of Pennsylvania and soon had his ventures up and running again. In 1882 he headed west to Chicago.

Yerkes' style, in his own words, was to "buy up old junk, fix it up a little, and unload it upon other fellows." This was surely something of an exaggeration, and Yerkes was not at all in the same class as King Mike McDonald. For one thing, he turned his ventures into operating mass transit services. But neither was Yerkes totally clear of charges that he used bribes to aldermen as backup to his ordinary business practices.

Yerkes did not have to be terribly omniscient to diagnose the ills of the Lake Street L. As with the South Side line—which turned handsome profits during the heavy traffic months of the Columbian Exposition but lost money continually thereafter—the absence of a true downtown terminal made the Lake Street line an ineffective competitor of the surface cars. Both elevated roads deposited their passengers on the edge of downtown Chicago, while the streetcar lines took them directly into the business district. It was also at this period in the early development of the elevated lines that the streetcar companies began to electrify their older horse and cable-powered vehicles, thus making available larger and faster streetcars and putting them in an even stronger competitive position.

Throughout the early 1890s it was continually suggested in many quarters, including several trade journals of the mass transit industry, that an elevated loop through and around the downtown business district would put the two elevated lines, as well as two more that were then abuilding, in sound fiscal shape. Most proposals envisioned an elevated right-of-way over which the existing L trains would operate. Other schemes projected a separate and independent elevated loop that would circumscribe the downtown business district and permit passengers to transfer to the main line elevated railways at interchange points. There was some daring talk about an underground loop subway and even an elevated moving sidewalk similar to one that operated at the Columbian Exposition. But while there was general acceptance of the idea that a downtown transit loop was what Chicago needed, the fulfillment of any of the specific proposals proved to be frustratingly difficult.[5]

CHAPTER THREE
Building the Loop

PERHAPS THE SINGLE most significant barrier standing in the way of a downtown loop elevated was an Illinois statute dubbed the "Adams Law." Named after its sponsor, Chicago state senator George E. Adams—a Union League Club member and active proponent of municipal reform—the law stipulated that any proposed elevated line that would be built over a public thoroughfare must obtain approval signatures from a majority of property owners along every mile of the route. Adams' purpose was to safeguard property owners against certain cavalier practices of the older streetcar companies that he, the senator, felt the emerging elevated companies would surely emulate. Actually, Chicago's 1872 city charter required *any* transit operator, streetcar or elevated, to secure approval signatures from a majority of property owners along any route on, or over, a public thoroughfare. In practice, however, the streetcar companies had become adept at balancing off collective opposition to a proposed route in a heavily settled area against approvals obtained from friendly property owners at the rural end of a line. The Adams Law, which applied only to elevated companies and not to streetcar lines, directed that approvals must be obtained from a majority of property owners within *each mile* of a proposed route.

The dual character of reaction to elevated construction on the part of property owners seems to be universal. Both residential and commercial property holders tend to welcome the improved transportation provided to an *area* by a new L, but rare is it that a home owner or retailer plumps for construction of a route over his own *street!* In 1887, as talk of elevated railways became ever more widespread in Chicago, [6] a group calling itself the West Chicago Protective League issued a pamphlet entitled *Opposition to Elevated Railways* which argued: "...the proposed elevated road would materially and irreparably depreciate the value of real estate upon said streets and their immediate vicinity, render the dwellinghouses (*sic*) thereon unfit for private residences, disturb and interfere with the public schools and scientific and charitable institutions and the worship of the congregations of the churches on the Sabbath and during the week, and wholly ruin said streets for foot travel or driving purposes."

Senator Adams' proposal was backed by the press and various reform groups, and became law on June 12, 1883. It was singularly responsible for encouraging the alley-L style of construction in Chicago, because it became common practice for abutters along a proposed elevated route to place a cash value on their approval signatures. (In 1895 the courts ruled such payments illegal, but it did not stop the practice.) "Civic associations" of various sorts were formed to insure that all property owners were kept informed of the going rates for approval signatures. In addition to straight payments *for* approvals, the reverse was not uncommon; the competitors of a proposed new route would offer payments to abutters provided they *refused* to sign an approval petition.

For their part, the elevated companies found that land acquisition costs for alley rights-of-way were less expensive and more predictable than outlays for approval signatures. As will be seen subsequently, the elevated railways of Chicago found themselves in very shaky financial positions virtually from the outset. This can easily be credited to the added construction costs imposed either through land acquisition or approval signature purchase—which the Adams Law, in essence, mandated. [7]

Given this very complex and delicate set of circumstances, Charles Yerkes had to play his hand with some care once he decided to push forward with the construction of a downtown loop. In the central business district of Chicago, land at premium prices eliminated any possibility of an alley L. Indeed, at one time thought was given to building an off-street elevated loop whose right-of-way would pass *through* major downtown office buildings at second-story level. Given the impracticality of this idea, if a loop elevated were to be constructed at all it would have to be over public thoroughfares. Yerkes would have to go through the approval signature process.

Of critical importance was the fact that Yerkes and his Philadelphia syndicate had begun yet another elevated railway venture, a line from downtown to the north and the northwest. This was incorporated in late 1893 and granted a city franchise early in 1894. Both it and his Lake Street line became toeholds for securing authorizations to build a loop distributor elevated line in downtown Chicago. Yet the way would still be tortuous.

On October 1, 1894, Yerkes obtained approval from the City Council to extend the Lake Street line 4,500 feet—less than a mile—eastward to Wabash Avenue. Property owners gave their consent, in other words, not to the initial leg of a loop but to the mere extension of an existing line. Then in June, 1895, Yerkes was able to secure a similar extension of his still unbuilt northwest elevated line. He obtained authorization to construct a line south of the Chicago River over Fifth Avenue, a thoroughfare today known as Wells Street. Now Yerkes met stiff opposition from Fifth Avenue abutters but, eventually, the lure of dollars was able to secure sufficient signatures. Another year of dealing and politicking went by before he was able to add a signed franchise for a Wabash Avenue leg of his proposed loop to his abuilding empire. At this juncture he formed a brand new company, the Union Elevated Railway, and no longer was there any pretense over the ultimate objective of the Yerkes syndicate. In his grand design, Yerkes saw the Union Elevated as a permanently separate company that would own the entire Loop elevated structure and trackage, although no rolling stock. Trains of the several elevated lines—the two under his control, plus two others—would use the new Loop and pay the Union Elevated a toll for each trip. However, when the Union Elevated was first incorporated, few believed that this latest scheme would fare any better than its numerous predecessors. The weekly trade newspaper *Engineering News* commented: "Some doubt may reasonably be felt as to the certainty of [the Loop's] immediate construction." Such doubts failed to take into account the consummate skills of Charles Tyson Yerkes, however.

A significant point is that both the Fifth Avenue and Wabash Avenue franchises authorized construction between Lake Street, on the north, and Harrison Avenue, on the south. The latter was thought suitable for the loop's southernmost and final lap, but Van Buren Street, two blocks north of Harrison, soon emerged as the more appropriate choice.

Ironically, it was from the abutters here that Yerkes ran into the most determined opposition. His answer was to organize yet another corporation, the Union Consolidated Elevated. Then he worked an interesting tactic out of the old streetcar companies' bag of tricks. Yerkes sought, and ultimately secured, a franchise for an elevated line over Van Buren Street that *could* extend over a mile, from Wabash Avenue all the way to Halstead. West of Fifth Avenue there was little hostility toward the proposed elevated line; large numbers of approval signatures were easily obtained. Not so along the half-mile stretch between Fifth and Wabash—the route needed to build the Loop's critical final leg—where there were property owners dead set on quashing Yerkes as well as his proposed L. Recall, however, that the Adams Law only required consent from a majority of property owners for each mile of franchise sought. Thus, Yerkes was able to get his majority on the basis of the abutters' support he received from west of Fifth Avenue—where he would never build an L! [8] Final City Council approval for the Van Buren leg of the Loop came through on June 30, 1896. Work was already underway on the previously approved Wabash, Fifth Avenue and Lake Street segments.

CHAPTER FOUR
The Metropolitan

ALMOST THREE YEARS after the South Side's inaugural, a third elevated company began operations in Chicago. Its original route commenced service on Monday, May 6, 1895, and linked downtown Chicago with residential neighborhoods to the west and northwest. During the early planning stage, it was taken for granted that this line would be steam powered, as were its two predecessors. It opened, however, as an electrified rapid transit line, for that new and silent energy source had meanwhile been sufficiently perfected for such heavy-duty installation. On inaugural day the first train, made up of a power car and two trailers, left Robey Street and Milwaukee Avenue bound for downtown Chicago at 6:00 A.M. One Thomas Hanson of 868 North Oakley was the first revenue passenger, for five cents.

On the early Metropolitan these power cars doubled as regular passenger-carrying vehicles and as locomotives capable of hauling as many as four non-powered trailers. The operation of several powered cars in a single train is standard procedure on all rapid transit lines today but it was an art that had yet to be perfected in 1895. All powered cars were also designated smoking cars, thereby making certain provisions for smokers on every train. On the steam-powered elevated lines smoking cars were a sometime thing, in fact nonexistent on the early South side, so that passengers were never sure they could indulge until they had checked out the consist of a given train. "The rolling stock of the road is of the finest grade," trumpeted the *Chicago Tribune* reporter assigned to the crack-of-dawn Metropolitan inaugural, an observation that was certainly read with satisfaction by officials of the Chicago-based Pullman Company, builders of the road's first trailer cars, and the Barney and Smith Car Company of Dayton, Ohio, which turned out a fleet of fifty-four wooden motor cars for the new electrified line.

With the eyes of Chicago starting to focus on the new downtown Loop elevated, the opening of the Metropolitan drew mixed reviews. While its trains would eventually operate onto the Union Elevated, when it opened in 1895 the line's "downtown" terminal was inconveniently west of the Chicago River at Canal and Jackson, prompting yet another reporter to note: "The part of the line in operation practically begins and ends nowhere."

This shortcoming was, fortunately, soon corrected. In just a few weeks the line had been extended outward to Logan Square, and inched closer to downtown Chicago via a massive four-track bridge over the Chicago River. Yet what remained an odd feature of the Metropolitan for over fifty years was that though the original line served residential neighborhoods to the *northwest* of downtown, it approached the business district on a circuitous route from the *southwest.*

An important fact to remember about the Metropolitan West Side Elevated Railroad (its official name) was that it was *not* part of the Yerkes empire. *The New York Times* saw fit to print that this was one of the new venture's two principal features, the other being its system of electrification. The *Times* spoke about "popular execration of the man who holds most of the Chicago street railways in his hand"—namely Yerkes—and commented most favorably about the young, dynamic and businesslike executives who were managing the Metropolitan.[9]

The system of electrification, not surprisingly, drew considerable national attention to the Metropolitan, for the West Side was the first rapid transit deployment of electricity in the United States on a scale beyond simple streetcar installations. Indeed, streetcar electrification itself was hardly tried and true technology when the West Side opened for business. Richmond, Virginia, in 1888 is generally credited with being the world's first successful streetcar electrification. The electrification of Chicago streetcar lines, a development which had an adverse competitive effect on the elevated lines, began in 1890. (By 1906 all horse and cable cars in Chicago had been converted to electric power.) Mainline railroading first adopted the new energy source in the same year the Metropolitan opened, when direct current locomotives began assisting steam engines on Baltimore & Ohio RR trains running through the Baltimore tunnels, hitherto chokingly smoke filled.

The West Side's power house—the company generated its own electricity—was a large red brick building located in an alley behind Throop Street, between Van Buren and Congress, and was topped off with an iron chimney a hundred and fifty feet tall. It was outfitted with fourteen self-stoking, coal-fired boilers. These supplied steam to a bank of four cross-compound vertical condensing engines with Corliss valves. These were directly coupled to four multipolar street railroad generators, two rated at 1500 kW and two at 800 kW each. The mechanical horsepower equivalent of the power station was proudly stated to be nine thousand.

Unlike standard transit electrification today, in which power is generated as alternating current, then converted to direct current in substations strung out along the line, the Metropolitan generated its electricity as direct current. The 600-volt charge was distributed to the line's motor cars through a third rail mounted 20⅛ inches outside, and 6¼ inches higher than, the regular steel running rails which were, of course, used for the "ground" of the electrical system. In a speech to the 1897 convention of the American Institute of Electrical Engineers in Eliot, Maine, M.H. Gerry of the Metropolitan claimed that his company generated electricity at a cost of one-half cent per kilowatt hour.

There was a further advantage realized by the company in converting to electricity. For steam locomotives operating through city neighborhoods, there was a municipal regulation that mandated the burning of anthracite coal. But with a stationary power house, the company could switch to cheaper bituminous, or soft coal, from nearby Illinois mines. Still other advantages, as continually pointed out by W.E. Baker, the general superintendent of the Metropolitan, included faster speeds, heavier trains, freedom from smoke and coal dust, less noise and a more convenient means of heating and lighting the cars. "We expect to save on operating expenses in two years the entire extra cost of the electric plant," Metropolitan vice-president E. F. Worcester told *The New York Times* in 1895.

The Metropolitan has a strong claim to be styled the world's first electrified rapid transit line, but there are purists who insist that a slight qualification is in order. Because, during the World's Columbian Exposition in Chicago, an installation called the Intramural Railway carried passengers on a three and one-half mile route around the fairgrounds. It was a genuine elevated system, it connected with the Alley L, and it was electrified. The powered cars drew current from a trackside third rail and hauled trailers just as would later be done on the Metropolitan. The system was dismantled at the close of the fair itself, but it was an important pilot project, and it helped insure the Metropolitan's later success.

Before the Union Loop opened in the fall of 1897, electric power had replaced steam on the Lake Street L. This happened in 1896. Then on August 16, 1897, President Leslie Carter of the South Side Rapid Transit Company petitioned the City of Chicago to allow his transit line to convert from steam to electricity, and the actual changeover took place shortly after the Loop opened. On both steam-to-electricity conversions, the wooden coaches previously hauled by steam engines were fitted out with electrical gear; totally new rolling stock was not required. The Lake Street followed the Metropolitan's practice of motorized cars hauling non-motorized trailers, but the South Side became the world's pioneer in the use of a brand-new system called "multiple-unit control," abbreviated "m.u."

The genius behind multiple-unit control was Frank Julian Sprague, Annapolis graduate and former associate of Thomas Edison. (Sprague's influence on mass transit cannot be overstated. It was he who engineered the world's first successful deployment of electricity in a streetcar system in 1888, for instance.) But Sprague's development of multiple-unit control has a particular Chicago twist. As the name implies, it is a system that enables trains of several motorized cars to be operated by one man from the leading car, the head end. All cars are thus self-powered; motorized power cars do not have to pull non-motorized trailers in locomotive-like fashion.

The idea which eventually germinated into m.u. control for electric railways had its origin in a control system for electric elevators that Sprague developed early in the 1890's. In 1897 Sprague was retained by the Alley L as a consultant on its pending steam-to-electricity conversion, the company's assumption being that a Metropolitan-like system of power cars and trailers would be used. Instead, the forceful Sprague convinced South Side management that a multiple-unit system would not only be superior, it was also quite possible. The company agreed to let Sprague give it a trial, although under the terms of a very restrictive contract that demanded results in a very short term. In July, 1897, Sprague successfully demonstrated m.u. control for the first time on a five-car test train along trackage beside the Erie Canal at the Schenectady works of the General Electric Company. Before the year was out he had demonstrated the invention on the Alley L itself, and by the middle of 1898 steam had been completely banished from the South Side Rapid Transit line—and soon thereafter, adopted by the other elevated lines in Chicago.[10]

Perhaps the best appreciation, not only of m.u. control but also of Sprague's daring in implementing his untried idea on the South Side,

A four-car elevated train on the Intramural Railroad that ran through the fairgrounds of the World's Columbian Exposition. This operation was the world's first electrified rapid transit service. (George Krambles Collection)

emerges in a letter that was written in 1932 on the occasion of Sprague's seventy-fifth birthday. The writer was one B.E. Sunny, a man who, in 1897, was the Chicago representative of the General Electric Company. G.E. fully expected to get the contract that eventually went to Sprague.

Writes Sunny: "I called on Mr. Hopkins, the general manager, one morning, expecting to receive the signed contract, but found him in rather bad humor. One of the directors had met a fellow in New York with a military title who had put in an electrically equipped dumb waiter, for delivering cocktails to the several floors of a big hotel, which worked perfectly, and he proposed to apply the same scheme to the operation of elevated trains. This seemed to us to be just too funny for anything, and we both had a good laugh over it."

But Mr. Sunny's laughter turned to dismay when he learned that "the name of the magician was Lieutenant Frank Sprague."

Sprague came to Chicago with no organization, no equipment, "just a toothbrush and an idea." But, as Sunny concluded in his birthday greeting thirty-four years later: "I am free to confess, dear Frank, that I did not give you favorable mention in my prayers at night. We lost the contract, you won, and it was a great day for railway transportation."

A final note on electrification: the replacement of steam power was encouraged by the favorable economics inherent in the new energy source. In Chicago, however, it got a political assist in a provision of one of Yerkes' franchise instruments for the Union Loop. The Wabash Avenue authorization stipulated that all trains using the Loop be electrically powered. A sole exception to the rule was that the South Side L could continue to use its steam engines for a period of three additional years only.

CHAPTER FIVE

The Loop Opens

CONSTRUCTION OF THE UNION LOOP went on through the summer of 1897, in spite of an extraordinary heat wave inflicting considerable discomfort on Chicago residents. The same summer saw a major outbreak of yellow fever in the southern United States; some cases were even reported as far north as downstate Illinois. On the shipping lanes of the North Atlantic, the American-flag passenger liner *St. Louis* captured the mythical Atlantic Blue Ribband from Hamburg American's *Furst Bismarck* with a crossing of six days, ten hours, fourteen minutes. Plans were also unveiled in the late summer of 1897 for a high-speed, grade-separated railway—a so-called "air line"—that would link Chicago and New York, achieving 100 mph speeds with electric cars of a radical, bullet-shaped design, powered by alternating current. In short, the dreamy springtime of the interurban era is at hand and electric-powered transportation appears to be the wave of the future.

The Lake Street L was first extended eastward onto, but not around, the Loop. By September, many inbound trains were continuing east on Lake Street past the turnoff for the line's original terminal at Market Street, concluding their runs at State and Lake.

On Labor Day, September 6, 1897, with neither announcement nor fanfare, Lake Street motor unit No. 101 and three trailer cars were taken out for a two-hour, three-circuit test trip around the new facility under the supervision of a motorman named John O'Brien. This was likely the first true operation around the entire circumference of the Union Loop. In fact, the decision to take the Labor Day ride had been made only two days earlier at a Saturday meeting. Lake Street General Manager Frank Hedley was asked by President DeLancey H. Louderback, Yerkes' chief executive, if a test ride were possible. Hedley, who would later become president of the Interborough Rapid Transit (IRT) in New York, said "yes," and company officials gathered at noon on the holiday for the outing. The press immediately speculated that regular passenger operations would follow in a matter of days.

It took somewhat longer. There were leases to be signed between the Union Elevated and the three other elevated companies then operating. Indeed, the South Side L had not even erected all the steel for its entry onto the Loop, although the concrete footings were in place. S.S.R.T. preferred to wait for final execution of its lease agreement before completing construction. Not until Friday, October 1, a whole month after the Labor Day test, did Federal Judge Showalter give his approval of a contract to allow the Metropolitan West Side to use the Loop. Necessary, because that company had by then gone into receivership and had to get court approval before entering into a contractual obligation.

The leases set the rates at which the Union would charge the Ls for the use of its Loop. These rentals were not slight, figured at a half-cent for every passenger carried, whether or not these riders boarded or departed trains at stations on the Loop. Furthermore, the Union was guaranteed a minimum income of $62,500 per elevated company per year, or a quarter million dollars when a fourth L (Yerkes' Northwestern Elevated), as yet uncompleted, would be connected to the facility. Thus, the Union

Elevated, with little in the way of day-to-day expense, could pay a guaranteed return of five percent on its five million dollars in preferred bonds. Yet the leasing lines were confident that with the efficient downtown distribution which the Loop would provide—increased patronage at five cents a ride—would make the toll supportable. Still, the Union Elevated was a classic example of watered stock, nineteenth-century style. It had issued five million dollars in bonds and an equivalent amount of common stock; yet total construction costs for the Loop elevated were estimated to be little more than $600,000.

On October 2, 1897, President Carter of the South Side L signed a lease with the Union Elevated.[11] There was, of course, no difficulty negotiating leases between the Union and Yerkes' two L companies, although it is interesting to note that the Northwestern Elevated, whose route was over three years away from completion, was required to pay an indemnity to the Union from the Loop's opening day as part of the arrangement by which it would have access to downtown Chicago.

October 3, 1897, was a quiet Sunday in Chicago, and at 7:00 A.M. on that otherwise inauspicious day, the first revenue train made its circuitious route around the Loop. It was a Lake Street train, and instead of terminating at Wabash and Adams as had lately been the practice, it continued south on Wabash along the Loop's outside track, turned west on Van Buren, north on Fifth Avenue (Wells Street), and then headed back to the L's western terminal after making another ninety degree turn at Fifth and Lake. The event took place without ceremony, nor was there any special ado nine days later, Columbus Day, when trains of the Metropolitan commenced schedules on the new facility in company with Lake Street trains. But at once there developed a characteristic that would haunt the Loop for all of its years—congestion: the Union Loop would be a crowded Loop as the participating Ls fed traffic into it, particularly during rush hours.

The *Chicago Tribune* assigned a reporter to ride the Loop during mid-afternoon that October 12th and report on his impressions. He was disappointed when it took twenty-five minutes to complete a circuit of the new facility, off seven minutes from the published schedules predicting that such a trip should take but eighteen minutes. Nevertheless, General

Opposite page: The Loop's intersection at Wabash and Van Buren was controlled by Tower 12. this 1899 view, a two-car Metropolitan train (left) passes a three-car Chicago & Oak Park (i. Lake Street) schedule. Remember—left-hand running. Also, early electrification on these rou used motorized power cars hauling non-motorized trailers. Look closely and see that only the le motorized cars were equipped with marker lights, head lamps, etc. (George Krambles Collectio

CABLE PIANOS
KIMBALL PIANOS
SILVERWARE
VOSE PIANOS
WEBER

Tower No. 8 was the interlocking facility that controlled the only entry point onto the Union Loop that no longer exists—Van Buren and Wells. Here, in the summer of 1937, a "Shopper Special" train from the Ravenswood line is turning onto Van Buren from Wells. Metropolitan West Side schedules entered and left the Loop over trackage continuing away from the photographer over Van Buren Street. (George Krambles Collection)

The "street columns" supporting Yerkes Union Loop, which caused such concern in 1897, are clearly evident in this contemporary view of the Wabash Avenue leg of the Loop.

Superintendent Baker of the Metropolitan said his company was "perfectly satisfied with the first day's experiment." Some Metropolitan employees failed to share Baker's satisfaction, however, and gave forth that the whole loop idea was "impractical and silly." Another professional source of negative opinion about the Loop emerged from among conventional railroad men. They seriously doubted that the proposed service levels of up to sixty trains an hour could ever be maintained. Their concern focused on the three junctions where the four elevated lines made their entry onto the Union Loop. Because all crossings were at grade, the L trains would forever be cutting in front of each other to the ruination of schedules, so the railroad men felt. Of course, "big railroad" people have never been comfortable with rapid transit and its close headways, and they aren't to this day!

Under-achievement in the matter of schedules was not the only comment voiced about the Union Loop. At street level, so to speak, serious criticism of the whole idea of constructing an elevated line over some of the city's major avenues continued to bubble and simmer. A "great public bother" and a "downtown nuisance" were two of the more gentle strictures. Despite the fact that Yerkes' construction authorizations from the City Council specified the use of lattice girders, through which some measure of

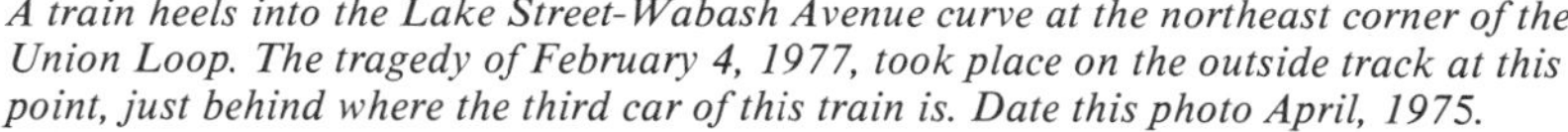

A train heels into the Lake Street-Wabash Avenue curve at the northeast corner of the Union Loop. The tragedy of February 4, 1977, took place on the outside track at this point, just behind where the third car of this train is. Date this photo April, 1975.

sunlight could illumine the streets below, many people objected to the comparative gloom which the elevated unavoidably inflicted on downtown Chicago.

The construction plan for the vertical support columns for the L likewise stirred up considerable ire. The reason? They were placed right in the street roadways. Union Loop officials had a rejoinder for such objections, however. They pointed out that the property owners signing approval petitions for the project clearly preferred street columns to the alternative course of action: columns right on the sidewalks, back from the curb line. The reason for this preference was that, rightly or wrongly, it was believed that the latter course would result in a structure of sufficient width for additional elevated trackage to be added at a later date. More overhead track was viewed as a far more objectionable future than support columns anchored in the roadways. As things turned out, the Van Buren Street portion did get built with columns along the sidewalk; thoroughfares Fifth Avenue, Wabash Avenue, and Lake Street got the street columns.

Objections to the elevated railway continued, however. One downtown retailer declared: "I have given up going to the North Western depot by carriage. I find that there is only one way practical—to walk." The gentleman was speaking of the route between his business establishment in the Loop and the North Western Railway terminal then located north of the Chicago River at Kinzie and Wells; traffic congestion brought about by the elevated's support columns inspired his complaint.[12] There was concern also expressed for the safety of pedestrians along Wabash Avenue between Madison and Randolph. Ever since 1892, a cable car line had operated in a "left-handed" fashion along this stretch; now it was feared that those columns holding up the Loop would obscure vision and thus, perhaps, contribute to mishaps by reason of pedestrians' lessened awareness of the surface cars.

But criticism or no, the Union Loop did open for business in the fall of 1897—and functions still! Lake Street and Metropolitan trains used the outside tracks and operated in clockwise direction. South Side service was assigned to the inside track and ran counter-clockwise, making the Union Loop a "left-hand running" operation, as in Great Britain. On the inside track, trains of a fourth L company would soon join the Alley L's.

For some long-vanished reason—and at this remove one can only wonder: whatever for?—a segment of the Chicago press kept referring to the Loop facility as the "Polly L." Mercifully, this nickname never took hold.

Lake Street leg of the Union Loop, 1977. The destination board of the lead 6000 series car reads, "Ravenswood."

Uneeda
Biscuit
5¢
LIMITED
357.

CHAPTER SIX

The Last L Company

THE OPENING OF THE NORTHWESTERN ELEVATED was preceded by events of a kind that legal beagles write articles about in law journals. It began with a franchise originally awarded by the City Council to Yerkes and his associates in 1894. The route to be built, basically due north from downtown into a number of growing residential communities, seemed a natural for rapid transit service. But throughout the line's construction delays occurred in the shape of strikes, material shortages, funding problems. In Chicago, as everywhere, transit franchise agreements stipulate a date by which service must begin; for the Northwestern three extensions would have to be voted by the City Council before the line could be completed.

The Yerkes syndicate actually began construction of the Northwestern before getting involved in the Lake Street L. Though the group was motivated by a desire to protect its own streetcar operations north of the Loop, a scarcity of willing investors for the project became an obstacle to fulfillment of this aim. The South Side Rapid Transit was at that time experiencing serious financial problems; also fresh in investors' memories was McDonald's plundering of the Lake Street venture. Nor had Yerkes himself yet convinced anyone that a Union Loop would ever be built in downtown Chicago. In 1896 work on the Northwestern ground to a halt for lack of sufficient capital. It would not be resumed for more than a year.

As the nineteenth century was expiring, so, likewise, was one of the Northwestern's franchises. December 30, 1899, fell on a Saturday. That day, the company energized the third rail along its route and declared that revenue service would begin the next day, yet with a warning that "of necessity the schedule will be irregular." The first train left the Lincoln Avenue station at 2:13 P.M. on December 31st. President Louderback said the departure at thirteen minutes after the hour caused him no concern, for "I am not a superstitious man," as perhaps he should have been in the light of future events. For the present, however, he averred as how this was "the proudest day of my life." The train of three cars, proclaimed by the Northwestern management to be the "finest products ever turned out by the Pullman company," was decorated with flags and bunting. At 2:33 P.M. it

Opposite page: Wells Street Terminal, circa 1922. Each of the four Chicago L companies operated a small stub-end terminal just shy of the Union Loop to handle overflow traffic that could not be accommodated on the downtown distributer. The Metropolitan West Side had this facility, which faced onto Wells Street between Jackson and Van Buren. In addition to being used by L trains, this terminal was also the Chicago terminal for Chicago, Aurora & Elgin interurbans. Train on the far right is such a service, about to head out over the Garfield L onto its "home rails" in Forest Park. (George Krambles Collection) entered the Loop under the control of the tower operator at Fifth and Lake. Tugboats in the Chicago River gave out with lusty salutes on their steam whistles, and Louderback proclaimed to those aboard as the train made its way around the Loop, "Well, boys, it's done."

Except it wasn't. Goading the company toward this New Year's Eve inaugural run was the fact that the Northwestern stood to forfeit $100,000 to the City of Chicago if service were not instituted before January 1, 1900. Officially, it was next up to the city's Commissioner of Public Works to inspect the company's project and recommend to the City Council that it be accepted in fulfillment of franchise requirements, a routine bit of business in normal circumstances. But when Commissioner L. H. McGann's staff started to give the new elevated line a careful going over they soon found it to be below par in many respects. Portions of the structure lacked the specified number of rivets, and only three out of fourteen stations were ready for passenger use. At 1:30 P.M. on New Year's Day the Chicago police ordered all work on the Northwestern to cease, including the operation of passenger trains. Mayor Carter C. Harrison, Jr., acting on the recommendations of Commissioner McGann and with the approval of Corporation Counsel Walker, had declared the franchise to be expired since the road was not in proper condition to commence service.

Attorneys for the traction company and the City of Chicago got to know each other well during the early months of 1900, during which a third and final extension of the franchise was negotiated. At last, on May 31, 1900, Pullman-built motor car No. 35, hauling trailers Nos. 197, 198 and 168, moved out of the Wilson Avenue yard of the new company and picked up a special contingent of VIPs for the road's "second inaugural." The train reached the Loop at noon, made a swift passage around the inside track of the downtown distributor and, with a motorman bearing the colorful name of H. du Flome skillfully manipulating the controls, headed back to the Wilson station on the westernmost track of the four-track elevated line.

Some distinguishing characteristics of the Northwestern: North of Chicago Avenue the line was built as a four-track facility to provide both local and express service. Additionally, during its early years the Northwestern practiced left-hand running in the British tradition, as did the Lake Street line and the Union Loop. Finally, the Northwestern's alley right-of-way was laid out with a number of sharp, twisting curves—a circumstance which plagues Chicago rapid transit to this day. The reason for this was rooted in the company's policy of acquiring real estate for its proposed line. After many parcels were secretly purchased through dummy corporations, property owners got wind of the transit developments and held out for higher prices. The Northwestern then decided to build a tortuously curved route over land it had already purchased rather than pay the rates property owners were demanding.

Following the inaugural trip, guests repaired to the Sheridan Park station of the Chicago, Milwaukee & St. Paul Railroad for a catered luncheon. The mayor of Chicago was represented by Commissioner McGann of the Department of Public Works, the man responsible for the road's shutdown on New Year's Day. There were speeches, accompanied by the rumble of elevated trains making their first revenue trips on the new line nearby. Yerkes predicted that with the advent of the full elevated network, the days of the street railways were over. He went on to suggest that some kind of unification of the several elevated operations would be a most desirable consummation. Yerkes also spoke with some feeling about yet another franchise dispute with the city, one that had bubbled up over some aspect of the Van Buren leg of the Union Loop, though the route was already in service. Since the city was demanding forfeit from Yerkes over the alleged non-fulfillment of a franchise stipulation, he said: "Even the City of Chicago has not the right to rob people, and the public does not want to see the money with which the city is run obtained by dishonest methods."

In due time the unification Yerkes called for on May 31, 1900, would take place—but not through any of Yerkes' doing. His welcome had worn thin in Chicago even before the Northwestern opened for business. In 1899 he attempted to secure a no-cost extension of one of his streetcar franchises that would be valid for a term of one hundred years. During the City Council debate a shouting mob surrounded City Hall demanding that Yerkes be repudiated. It was said he had handed out over a million dollars in bribes to secure favorable action on the measure. To no avail; the proposal was voted down. Yerkes eventually sold his Chicago traction interests and moved to New York. Later he removed across the North Atlantic to London, where he formed a syndicate that built three important tube lines in the British capital.[13] Charles Tyson Yerkes died in 1905 at the age of sixty-eight.

In common with many who helped build Chicago's elevated system, Yerkes is all but forgotten today; there are no memorials to him in Chicago. Or elsewhere, except for an observatory a hundred miles from State and Madison, in Williams Bay on Lake Geneva, Wisconsin, which he endowed in 1892. Students of American literature are not likely to be familiar with the historical Yerkes, but they will surely be aware of Frank Algernon Cowperwood, the principal figure in three famous Theodore Dreiser novels: *The Financier*, *The Titan*, and *The Stoic*. Cowperwood is Yerkes

The shape of things in 1900, in which an open-platform car of Yerkes' Northwestern Elevated Railroad crosses Chicago Avenue—destination, Loop—hauling two non-motorized trailers. Like the Lake Street line, the Northwestern operated British style, left-hand running. (George Krambles Collection)

virtually to the life. So closely did Dreiser model Cowperwood on Yerkes that, in the absence of a true biography of the man, *The Dictionary of American Biography*, in an article written by Max Lerner and Mary Holler, recommends the Dreiser trilogy for those who would like to learn more about Yerkes.

Over the ensuing decades, the several elevated companies continued to expand, generally independent of each other, and especially independent of the various streetcar lines. Despite the interest initially expressed by Yerkes and his syndicate in operating surface and elevated lines jointly, this did not come to pass. They remained in competition with each other throughout the first half of the twentieth century.

Such expansion as the elevated companies pursued after the opening of the Northwestern in 1900 was chiefly in the construction of more and deeper tap roots into residential communities surrounding the downtown core. By so doing they exercised a pronounced influence on the growth of the city and the region. Only the elevated lines were able to provide tolerable (and inexpensive) commuting times between downtown Chicago and new residential developments that began to spring up in outlying communities like Ravenswood and Rogers Park to the north, Berwyn and Cicero to the west, and Washington Park to the south. But perhaps more important was the effect of the Union Loop on the city's downtown business district. Major office buildings, department stores, public agencies and railroad terminals were built in—or immediately adjacent to—the rectangle formed by Lake, Wabash, Van Buren and Fifth/Wells. As a result, the City of Chicago has since had one of the most concentrated downtown business districts of any American city. Likely it always will.

Peaceful retirement. At the Illinois Railway Museum in Union, Illinois, two vintage elevated line cars have been lovingly restored, and carry tourists over museum trackage. Car 1024 is an open-platform unit that was built for Yerkes' Northwestern L by Pullman, in 1898. Car 1808 is an enclosed platform unit originally built as a non-motorized trailer at the turn of the century. In 1913 it was converted to a motor car. Both old-timers saw action through the CRT regime. (George Krambles Collection)

Notes to Part One

[1]Additional details on these cars, as well as all Chicago transit equipment from 1892 through 1947, can be found in: *Chicago's Rapid Transit*: Volume I, Rolling Stock, 1892–1947. (Chicago: Central Electric Railfan's Association, 1973).

[2]The World's Columbian Exposition commemorated the 400th anniversary of the discovery of the New World by the famed Italian navigator. The incomplete fairgrounds were, in fact, opened on October 12, 1892. They were quickly closed again for the winter months, and then re-opened for a full season in the spring of 1893.

The new elevated railway was not the only novel transport scheme unveiled for downtown-to-fairgrounds travelers. Among several waterborne services was a new and different passenger vessel built by Alexander McDougall, one of the Great Lakes premier shipbuilders. His S.S. *Christopher Columbus* carried two million passengers during the 1893 season, but is more notable in being the only passenger vessel ever built with a "whaleback" hull. The whaleback design was developed by McDougall and achieved some popularity on Great Lakes bulk freighters. It featured a sausage-like hull that, with its superstructure removed, looked like a big floating log!

Aficionados of pageantry still regard the World's Columbian Exposition as the grandest world's fair of all time.

[3]The so-called Meigs Elevated Railway, a steam-powered monorail that employed cylindrical cars and which never advanced beyond modest experimental deployment in Cambridge, Massachusetts.

[4]Although its focus is primarily Chicago's street railways, and the elevated companies to a lesser extent, an interesting study of political corruption in the arena of public transportation is: Robert David Weber, *Rationalizers and Reformers*: Chicago Local Transportation in the Ninteenth Century. (Ann Arbor, Mich.: University Microfilms, 1971).

Two scenes from a breakthrough in the development of electric traction railroading: Above, Schenectady, N. Y., July 26, 1897. Frank Sprague is running tests of his novel system of multiple-unit control (see note 10, page 41). Six wooden South Side Rapid Transit L cars have been sent east for the important experiments. Lead car, No. 130, is a Gilbert Car Company product built in 1892 for use behind South Side steam locomotives and later electrified. Opposite page: Sprague demonstrated the first m.u. operation on the South Side itself, April 15, 1898. The picture is a view two days later as he and his co-workers continue to perfect the operation. (Both pictures from George Krambles Collection)

[5]It is not known precisely how the idea of an elevated transit loop around Chicago's business district germinated. It is possible several street-level loops which the cable railways employed served as technical prototypes. When the cable cars were at their zenith, there were five separate turnaround loops in downtown Chicago, most being just a few blocks in size. As noted earlier, these cable car loops gave rise to the practice of calling downtown Chicago "the Loop."

Also it is sometimes claimed that a rapid transit facility circumscribing a downtown business district is unique to Chicago, but this is not so. Since October, 1884, London has been girded by the Inner Circle line, a combination subway and surface transit route fed by other lines leading out into residential areas. Glasgow opened a downtown tube line in 1897 that remains to this day an independent operation, not linked to any other transit lines. It is simply a circular or loop distributor around the downtown zone. Until 1936 this line was cable powered; it now operates electrical equipment much like the tube lines of London.

[6]The first reasonably serious proposal to build an elevated railway in Chicago dates to 1869, when a group attempted to secure a charter to construct such a line over State Street southward out of the downtown area. By the end of the nineteenth century, as many as seventy separate proposals had surfaced from one quarter or another.

[7]The Lake Street L was the only one of the early Chicago lines to forgo alley construction and be built over a city thoroughfare in its entirety. Others, including the original South Side L, employed street construction here and there, but only Lake Street had no alley construction at all. The Lake Street L was also identified with bribes and corruption during its early years, thus lending weight to speculation that the organizers used their influence with the City Council to circumvent the full intent of the Adams Law. By its own admission, the City Council did approve elements of the Lake Street franchise without proper approval signatures being submitted. See Weber, *Rationalizers and Reformers*, pages 177–224.

[8]The Metropolitan West Side Elevated, a company not under Yerkes control, will construct its entry onto the Union Loop over two blocks of Van Buren Street west of Fifth Avenue/Wells Street.

[9]Two notable people whose transit careers began on the Metropolitan: Britton I. Budd, who became president of all Chicago elevated railways during the Samuel Insull era; and William S. Menden, a young man who designed much of the company's early rolling stock, and later became the chief officer of the Brooklyn-Manhattan Transit Corporation (BMT) in New York.

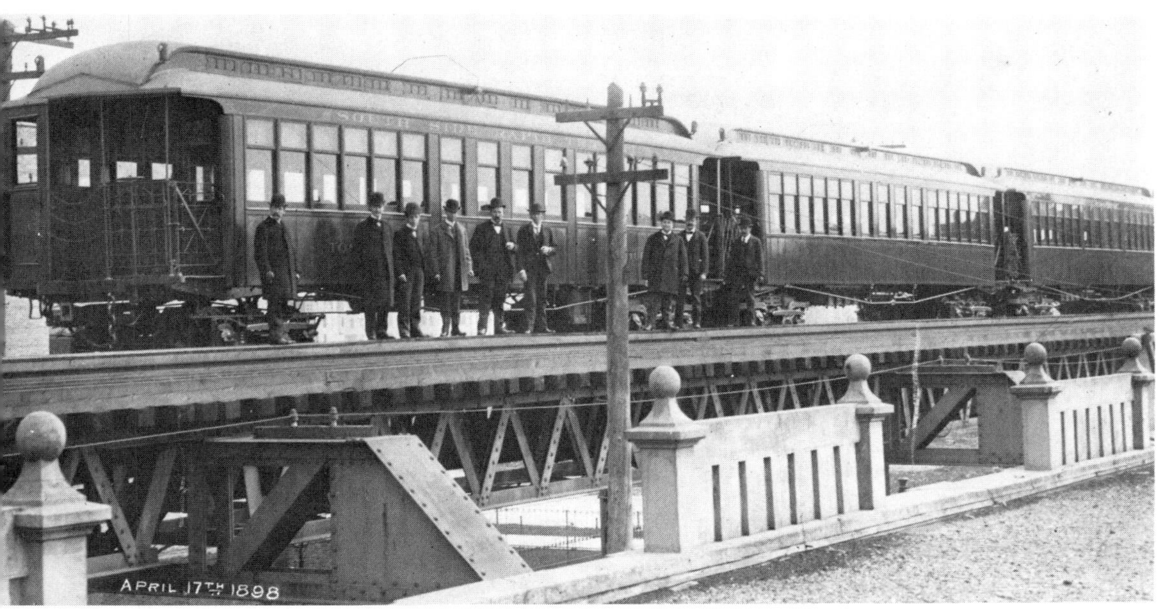

[10]With motors on each car, a train of any length automatically has the proper amount of tractive force, neither too much or too little, and there is no mechanical inefficiency in making trains shorter or longer as traffic warrants. Thus the *motivation* for m.u. control.

It *works* like this: traction motors on each car are fed electricity by a motor controller, so called, a device located under each car that opens and closes the correct electrical circuits for various speed, and direction, settings. Today, motor controllers are cam-like devices that look not unlike the tuner in a television set, only larger. In years gone by they were sets of switches and relays.

The motor controller is activated by a low voltage control circuit. When the motorman at the head end of a multi-car train applies power, what he actually does is feed low voltage into the motor controllers on all the cars, thus causing the motor controllers to feed high voltage from the third rail into the traction motors in the same fashion and simultaneously. Third-rail current is thus not passed from one car to the next; only the low voltage control circuits must be bridged from car to car. In the early days this was done with jumper cables that had to be manually connected when cars were coupled; today it is normally accomplished automatically by contact buttons built into the couplers.

For an account of multiple-unit control written less than a decade after Sprague perfected the procedure, see: Sidney Alymer-Small, *Electrical Railroading*. (Chicago: Frederick J. Drake and Company, 1908), pages 657–668.

[11]Unlike the Metropolitan, the South Side L was not in receivership in October, 1897, but it had been recently through receivership and had not paid a dividend in some time. In September, 1896, the company was unable to meet interest payments on its bonds and was put up for public auction at the Cook County Courthouse. Stock which had once sold for $100 a share had dropped to the $1.50 range. In December, 1896, no less a nabob than J. P. Morgan was rumored to be interested in purchasing the Alley L, but nothing ever eventuated.

[12]Substitute "bus" or "taxi" for "carriage," and this lament could easily be voiced today in Chicago by homeward bound commuters trying to catch Chicago & North Western trains. In 1906, H.G. Wells described Chicago streets as ". . .simply chaotic—one hoarse cry for discipline!"

[13]The Bakerloo, Northern and Picadilly lines, three important links in London Transport's rail network. For further details on this period of Yerkes' career, see: T.C. Barker and Michael Robbins, *A History of London Transport*, Volume II: The Twentieth Century. (London: George Allen and Unwin, Ltd., 1974).

[14]All three novels were originally published by the World Publishing Company, of Cleveland and New York: *The Financier* (1912), *The Titan* (1914), and *The Stoic* (1947). *The Titan* deals with the Chicago phase of Cowperwood's career and his exploits in the traction industry.

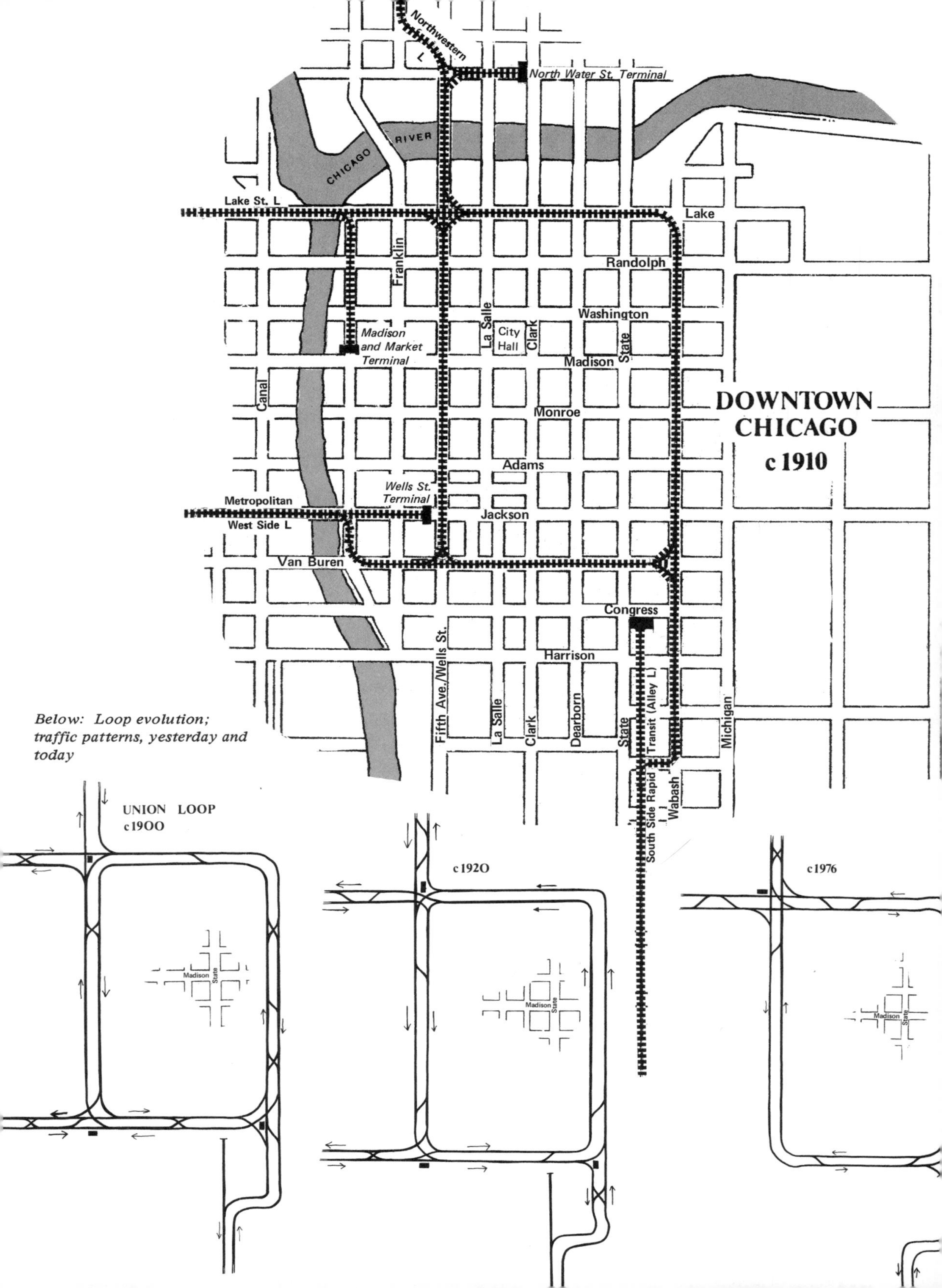

Below: Loop evolution; traffic patterns, yesterday and today

PART TWO

The Subway

CHAPTER SEVEN

The Insull Imprint

DESPITE THE POPULARITY which the Loop L quickly attained, there were those in Chicago who felt that the entire business was a terrible mistake right from the start. "That Chicago should be forced to endure such an outmoded arrangement speaks very little for this city's civic imagination," lamented one commentator. An underground subway, it was argued, would have better suited the city's needs.

Subways, of course, were in their infancy when the Union Loop opened in 1897. But it was an infancy that precociously sprouted to full adulthood after the turn of the century. The world's very first was a steam-powered line that opened in London in 1863. It hauled some of Queen Victoria's subjects over a 3.7-mile track—chokingly smoke-infested—between Farringdon Street and Bishop's Rock, Paddington. America waited until the advent of electric traction before building transit lines beneath the ground. On September 1, 1897, open-bench trolley cars of Boston's West End Street Railway began ferrying passengers into the nation's first subway, adjacent to historic Boston Common. New York inaugurated service on the first line of what would become the largest subway system in the world on October 27, 1904. Philadelphia opened its Market Street line, subway–elevated, in 1908. That same year William Gibbs McAdoo began running trains of his Hudson and Manhattan Railroad Company under the mighty Hudson River between New York City and Hoboken, New Jersey.[1]

"It's the straphangers who pay the dividends," Charles Yerkes was reputed to have once said. Chicago Ls still seemed short of cars in 1908, when John T. McCutcheon drew this cartoon, "The Traction Magnate's Dream." (Author's collection)

Preceding page: Trains bound for CTA's State Street subway leave the old South Side elevated alighment near Roosevelt Road and dip into the underground tube. Elevated line in background saw Chicago's very first L operation in June, 1892.

Whereas political and civic leaders in Chicago were willing to talk about a subway, the original operators of the four elevated lines viewed such a possibility with slightly less alarm than the plague. Underlying their apprehension was the grim reality of subway construction costs, some four to six times greater than an elevated line. Although Boston and New York used municipal funds to construct their underground tunnels, the L operators had no assurance that such generosity would prevail in midwestern Chicago. Consequently any subway lines would likely involve private capital—*their* capital.[2] The elevated companies thus closed ranks against any sentiment for building subways, whether it made sense to do so or not. Returning from a trip to Europe in 1897, Charles Yerkes pontificated that "the underground system is quite satisfactory, I believe, in cities like New York, where the sewerage is good; but in cities where the sewerage is in the least particular faulty the system is impractical." On another occasion, Yerkes dismissed the idea of a subway with this sociological observation: "Chicago wants the crowds on its streets. It wants the bustle and the excitement which they bring." Again, he made it even more dogmatic: "The underground arrangement would not be practical at all in Chicago." Thus, three strikes against subways from the top L man in town!

Interestingly, Yerkes' protestations were running squarely in the face of an overwhelming body of facts. For the truth is that by the turn of the century, Chicago had become downright famous for its various underground tunnels, tunnels built for all sorts of diverse purposes. As far back as 1866 a five-foot diameter tube was completed from the shore line out into Lake Michigan. It was used to bring drinking water into the city.

After the Great Fire of 1871, additional underground water conduits, including sewers, were built, many of a size comparable to a subway tunnel. Vehicular and pedestrian tunnels under the Chicago River predate the 1871 fire, and were used to good advantage by people fleeing that holocaust. Indeed, in order for the cars of the various cable railways to cross the Chicago River and gain entry to downtown Chicago from either the north or the west, where the river serves as a sort of moat, subaqueous tunnels were necessary. The bridges all opened to permit the passage of river traffic, and it was not possible for movable bridges to accommodate underground conduits for the endlessly traveling cables. (During the beginning days of the cable cars, before all tunnels were completed, cars on some routes disengaged from the cable shy of the river and were hauled over the bridge and through downtown Chicago by horses.)[3] In 1901 work was begun on Chicago's totally unique underground freight tunnels, a system that grew to sixty-two miles of single track, underground, narrow-gauge railway in the downtown area by the year 1909, described later herein.[4]

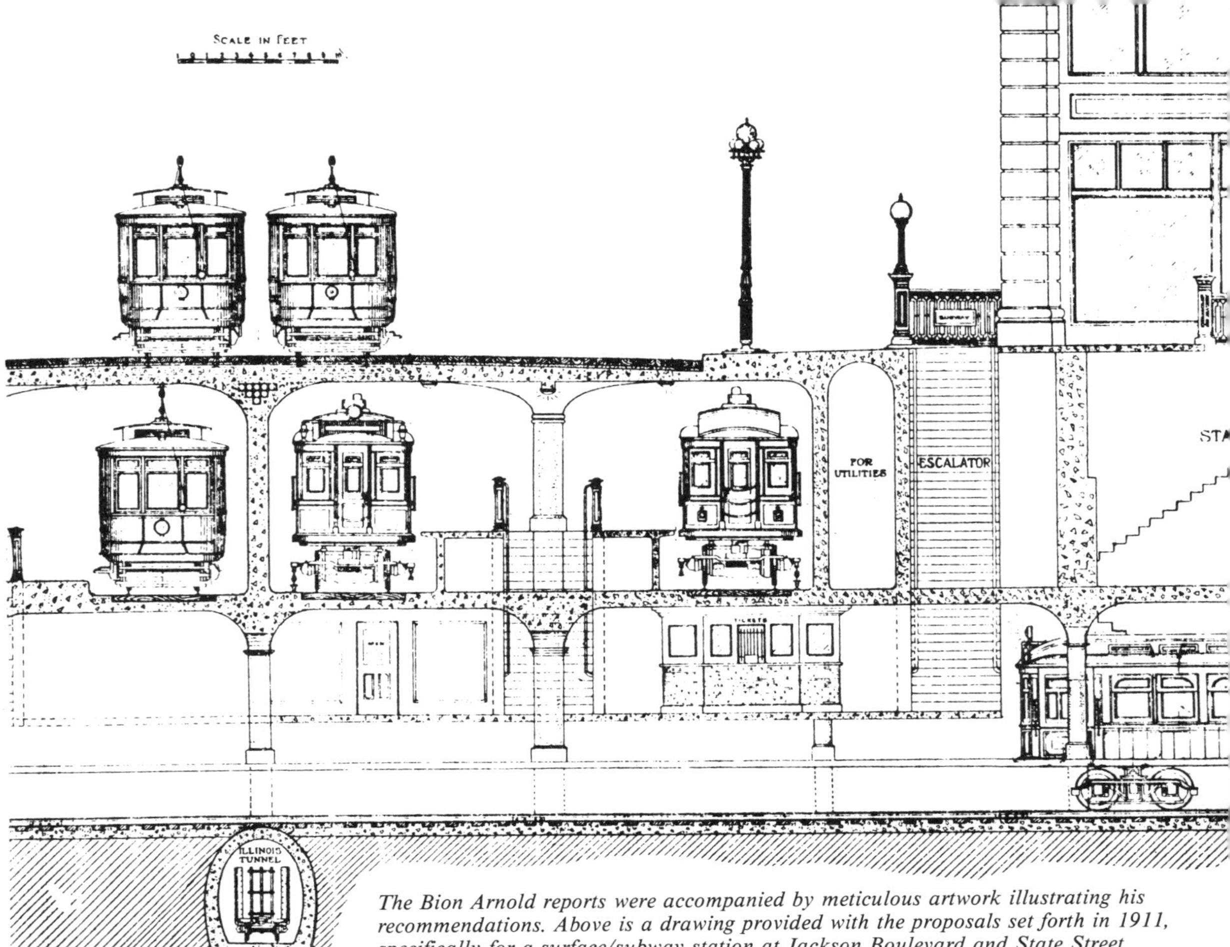

The Bion Arnold reports were accompanied by meticulous artwork illustrating his recommendations. Above is a drawing provided with the proposals set forth in 1911, specifically for a surface/subway station at Jackson Boulevard and State Street. Note inclusion of the "Illinois Tunnel," left, to be described in Chapter Fifteen. (Author's collection)

Small wonder, then, that despite the desire of the elevated companies to squelch such talk, discussion of subway transit lines never petered out in Chicago. In 1902, Bion J. Arnold, an engineer of considerable reputation, made a now-famous report to the Committee on Local Transportation of the Chicago City Council, which strongly recommended the construction of a downtown subway system. In 1911 more proposals were put forth, and in 1916 a voluminous report was jointly prepared by Arnold, Robert Ridgeway and William Barclay Parsons, chief engineer for the construction of New York's original IRT subway. This advocated a comprehensive subway system that both elevated trains and streetcars would use.[5]

The more the elevated companies persisted in their anti-subway posture, the more the city's political leadership attempted to exploit the natural competition between the Ls and the surface cars by turning to the idea of underground tunnels which would bring the city's streetcar lines into the heart of downtown Chicago with much greater dispatch than they managed at street level. A most important fact about Chicago public transportation in the post-Yerkes era is that the elevated and surface lines were, indeed, genuine competitors of each other. Quantitatively, the surface lines transported considerably more passengers than the elevateds. In 1906, for instance, the Ls carried 132 million passengers, while the surface lines carried 402 million. In 1916 the ratio was 181 million passengers on the elevated lines to 686 million on the streetcars.

Because of this competition, the cable cars and their successor trolley lines were never interested in a "feeder line" role vis-à-vis the elevated system. Why give away fares? Rather they sought to retain and promote their own direct services between downtown Chicago and the various residential neighborhoods. Such services—and the lines' competitive position—would be markedly improved were they to have access to underground tunnels in the more congested areas.

The rival managers of the surface lines and the elevated companies were aware of their respective positions. Since it was the political establishment that was always talking about grandiose new transit projects, a proper cultivation of the city's elected officials was viewed by transit management as a businesslike bulwark against sudden and unexpected developments. A useful means the companies employed to keep the attention of local politicians focused where they wanted it was labor patronage. It was not unusual for a member, or members, of the City Council to have first call on large numbers of jobs on either the elevated lines or the surface routes. Sometimes both! In 1910, the *Chicago Daily News* quoted an L official's remark about an alderman from the city's eighth ward: "We have put all of his people to work on our road yet it seems all the more does he want to drive us from business."[6]

Ordinary common sense, however, impelled movement in the direction of transit unification in Chicago, unification not only of the separately managed elevated lines with each other, but with the surface lines as well.[7] Finally, one actual effort to achieve such an amalgamation brought Samuel Insull into the rapid transit business.

Young English-born Samuel Insull would, in our time, have achieved "gifted child" status; in his own era, that of Victorian England from 1859 onward, he must have been recognized as a prodigy, if not immediately a genius. At any rate, when only fourteen he was employed as a secretary, eventually to toil in this capacity for the British representative of Thomas A. Edison. At twenty-two he became private secretary to the great Edison himself, migrating to America in 1881 to do so. Such was Insull's

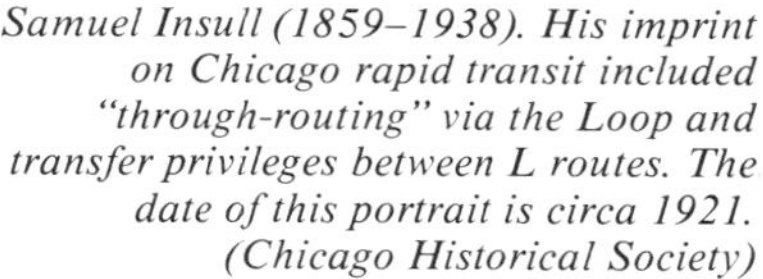

Samuel Insull (1859–1938). His imprint on Chicago rapid transit included "through-routing" via the Loop and transfer privileges between L routes. The date of this portrait is circa 1921. (Chicago Historical Society)

gift for synthesizing concepts and quantities of data into workable business operations that within ten years he was managing the whole of Edison's commercial enterprise.

1892—when the South Side L opened—was also the year Insull came to Chicago to embark on a career as one of the remarkable movers and shakers in American industry, public utilities division. When the bulk of the Edison companies melded with rivals to form the General Electric Company, Insull was offered a vice-presidency. Instead, he chose to become president of the then struggling Chicago Edison Company. This modest steam-powered, electricity generating operation thus became Insull's steppingstone to an industrial and personal power base of vast dimensions, totaling upward of 2.5 billion dollars in assets and comprised of steam and hydroelectric generating plants, plus distribution networks, in thirty-two states.

Though electric railways would be a very, very small segment of the total Insull empire, in Chicago, at least, they would be a highly visible part. As he tells it himself in his *Memoirs*, Insull's participation began in 1911.[8] Henry A. Blair was then in control of what had evolved into Chicago's two principal streetcar companies. He asked Insull to join him in an effort to unify all Chicago mass transit, surface as well as elevated. Following Yerkes' exit from the transit stage, a reasonably strong public sentiment in favor of total municipal operation of Chicago mass transit had made itself felt, and was reinforced by dissatisfaction over slowly deteriorating L service. Mayor Fred Busse, who served between 1907 and 1911, did much quiet behind-the-scenes work to restore at least a potential for renewed public confidence in privately operated trains and trolleys, and the Blair-Insull approach seemed sensible.

This was based on awareness that the elevated companies were the weak lines in the proposed unification—by comparison, the surface lines were in better fiscal shape. Therefore new capital must be secured for the Ls with which to finance the merger with the surface lines. Working through the Insull-controlled Commonwealth Edison Company, loan guarantees for six million dollars were established and assigned to a voluntary association of the four L companies, together named the Chicago Elevated Railways Collateral Trust.

To no avail; the elevated lines were unable to meet the interest payments on these new loans. When they defaulted, Insull himself became the principal stockholder in the four companies—a transit magnate, no less! Furthermore, because of the default the elevated companies became an ever less desirable merger partner for Blair's surface lines, and the idea of total transit unification went into eclipse.

Changes to the Loop

For his chief operating officer, Insull reached into the ranks of the Metropolitan. Acting on the suggestion of that line's chairman, Frederic A. Delano, Insull selected 41-year-old Britton I. Budd to become president of each of the four elevated companies. Budd was supported by Insull himself, in his capacity as chairman of the board of directors of each company. Thus, while the proposed merger with the surface lines failed to materialize, Samuel Insull took charge of the four elevated companies and gave them a de facto sort of unification through a common chief officer. Some would even say that under Insull the elevated companies of Chicago had their finest hour. Eventually, in 1924, the separate companies were formally unified into a single entity, the Chicago Rapid Transit Company, the CRT.[9]

Prior to this, however, in the early days of Insull's control a system of "through-routing" was put into effect over the Union Loop. This policy included free transfers between trains of the four lines. Until this time, passengers had to pay separate fares for each ride, and trains of the four companies stopped at segregated positions along the Loop.

The through-routing scheme brought about a major operating change to the Loop. Up to 1913, operation on the two-track structure was in both directions—clockwise on the outside track, counterclockwise on the inside. In order to allow Northwestern trains to be through-routed onto the South Side line, and vice versa, the Loop was made over into a "one-way street," so to speak; all trains, on both tracks, would run in the counterclockwise direction. To facilitate this changeover, both the Northwestern and the Lake Street elevateds—the latter by now renamed the Chicago & Oak Park—gave up their British-style running in favor of the American "right hand" standard.

Physical and technical alteration to the Loop L itself included either the replacement or relocation of signals and switches, and the construction of footbridges to connect inner and outer platforms. At the parlimentary and bureaucratic levels, there was much to-do. The City Council busied itself with the creation and enacting of ordinances amending old franchise agreements; officialdom launched an intensive public education program to acquaint L patrons with the ins and outs of the new, through-routing dispensation.

November 1, 1913, was a football Saturday, during which the University of Chicago would beat the University of Illinois, 28 to 7, at Stagg Field. Earlier that morning a test train left Jackson Park on the South Side line and operated through to Wilmette, the community at the very northernmost point of the Northwestern L. As it passed through the Loop, workmen there were still putting the final touches on the downtown facility in anticipation of the start of regular through service. Aboard the special—work trains excepted, it was the first to operate from one line onto the other—were Britton Budd, Samuel Insull, other company officials, and representatives of the various Chicago newspapers.

Insull expressed regrets that such a through-routing arrangement had not been instituted "years ago," and was most convincing when he insisted to reporters that the new system would mean "no financial advantage" to his companies. Nay, it was simply a necessary civic betterment for the people of Chicago, Insull claimed.

Actually, through-routing would involve a relatively few trains each day, and the great majority of Northwestern and South Side trains would continue to terminate in downtown Chicago and then head back to their terminals of origin. The biggest advantage which the new system would bring to the public was the privilege of transferring freely from one line to another on the Loop. On the following Monday, November 3rd, congestion at several downtown stations of the Union Loop amply demonstrated that the new arrangement was most effective in doing exactly what it was designed to do: woo passengers away from the surface cars, where the practice of line-to-line transfers had long been in effect, onto the elevated lines. Insull's declamations about "no financial advantage" were quite untrue. Once it became apparent that the proposed 1911 elevated-surface unification would not take place, Insull had reshaped his strategy, concentrating instead on improving the competitive posture of the elevated lines vis-à-vis the trolleys. The shift was clearly dictated by business acumen, not civic altruism.

The "universal transfer system," as it came to be called, was scheduled to begin at 12:01 A.M. on Sunday. Then, when a large crowd of "Saturday nighters" appeared to take advantage of the new system, it was, with President Budd's on-the-spot authorization, actually put into effect an hour early, at the Fifth and Randolph L station on the Loop. The first through-routed train in revenue service left Wilmette at 5:37 A.M. on Monday, November 3rd. It was due to reach the Loop at Fifth and Lake—the entry point to the Union facility controlled by Tower 18—at 6:38. Confusion associated with the changeover caused the inaugural to run late, so that it didn't get to the Loop until after seven o'clock.

Under Budd's management, the four elevated companies—and after 1924 their single successor, the CRT—were not turned into dividend-paying components of the far-flung Insull empire. But they were smartly managed, and they performed with distinction. It is even questionable whether Blair's suggestion for a combined surface-elevated network, which first triggered Insull's interest in electric traction in 1911, was taken up by Insull primarily for its profit potential. (He also sallied into the field of electric interurban railways, as will later be told, but his entry into that area of transportation was motivated by old-fashioned business interest.) With regard to the elevated lines, though, it is more likely that Insull was principally interested in improving the performance and image of what was, after all, Commonwealth Edison's largest customer! Now that electric utilities had become a growth element in the overall economy, it simply would not do to have the highly visible Chicago elevated railway lines—*electrified* elevated lines—continually regarded as financial and operational problems. "Who ever heard of el (*sic*) stock paying dividends?" queried Insull when, after he had outlined his plans for improving the elevated roads, a reporter asked him how this would affect the bottom line.[10]

In any event, CRT benefited from the Insull imprint. The four elevated companies were anything but robust in the post-Yerkes era and, had not a Samuel Insull happened along to put them under his protective wing, they surely would not have survived. Which is to say they would likely have become public wards of one sort or another, and while this eventually

STEEL CARS FROM THE INSULL ERA

Above: Steel cars from the Insull era saw their last service in the early 1970s on the Evanston Express service. It's the morning rush hour, and commuters are heading for their offices.

Below: A group of 4000 series cars sits in CTA's Wilson Yard in early 1974, shortly after having been withdrawn from regular service.

happened after the collapse of the Insull empire, it is probably well that it took place later rather than sooner.

The collapse of the Insull empire during the Great Depression was a mighty fall. Insull himself had not salted away a personal fortune immune from the fate of his enterprises, so he lived out his final years on a small pension. Since one of his chief strategies had been to solicit small investments from people of modest means, many saw their life savings wiped out when Middle West Utilities, Insull's key holding company, entered receivership in 1932. Insull himself, then a man of seventy-three years, headed for Europe and a retirement that would be far from peaceful and idyllic.

In October of that year, after he left Chicago, Insull was indicted on charges of embezzlement and of using the mails to defraud investors. There followed eighteen months of endeavor to bring the aging tycoon back to America to stand trial.

Insull had settled in Greece, and while Greek courts at first refused to honor the United States government's petitions to have him extradicted, it became apparent in early 1934 that his about-to-expire visa would not be renewed. In March he slipped quietly out of Athens aboard an old 1700-ton tramp steamer, the S. S. *Maiotis*, that had been chartered for Insull by an English friend. First he headed for Persia, then changed course and made for the Black Sea coast of Rumania. Rumania was unwilling to allow Insull ashore and announced he would be arrested if he so much as essayed a landing. Turkish authorities halted the *Maiotis* in the Bosporus and took the industrialist ashore to languish for a number of days and nights in a miniscule cell in an Istanbul jail—he who, not many months past, had been the lord and master of a 5,000-acre estate in Libertyville, Illinois.

In due course the Turkish courts acceded to the United States' petition for extradition. Insull was released to American authorities on April 13, 1934—a Friday—for the long voyage home, aboard the steamship *Exilona* of the American Export Line. *The New York Times* noted, editorially, the obvious similarities between the voyages of Insull and Odysseus.

In the early morning of May 7, 1934, the *Exilona* came abreast of *Ambrose* lightship outside New York Harbor, and was met there by the Coast Guard cutter *Hudson*. The *Hudson* took the famous fugitive to Sandy Hook, where Samuel Insull set foot on American soil once more at 8:15 A.M. Eastern Daylight Saving Time. Transported by fast motorcade across New Jersey to Princeton Junction, the party boarded a westbound Pennsylvania Railroad train. Insull, together with his captors, traveled in a private car and arrived in Chicago's Union Station the next morning.

After all this doing, Insull was acquitted on all counts! He returned to Paris after his trial, where he died on July 16, 1938, four months short of his seventy-ninth birthday.

As for the Chicago Rapid Transit during this period, it did not fare well. Like the other Insull enterprises it was forced into receivership. On June 28, 1932, Judge Wilkerson of the United States District Court acted in response to a creditor's petition and appointed receivers for the ailing company. The great bulk of the Insull empire would eventually emerge from receivership as the nation fought its way out of the Depression, but the CRT would regain stability only when it became a public authority after World War II.

Meanwhile, in New York, that city's subway system was growing in size and reputation, capped by the opening, in 1932, of the municipally-operated Independent Subway. Here was an achievement Chicagoans might well envy, as the Loop L strained under the press of ever increasing traffic. The 1930 census tallied 3.4 million as the city's population, exactly double what it had been in 1900. This growth, plus patronage from outlying communities in suburban Cook County, brought the L's annual passenger total up to 183 million, from seventy-six million just two decades earlier.

Again there was talk about a subway and—away with the Union Loop!

CHAPTER EIGHT
A New Deal for Chicago

UNDER INSULL the elevated companies backed off from their negative stand on the notion of a downtown subway. In fact, they were moved toward a genuinely supportive position on the idea, although Insull himself often expressed the view that political considerations seemed to prevent Chicago forever from getting started on any such project. On the day before Insull and Budd entertained reporters on that first through-routed L train in 1913, Chicago mayor Carter H. Harrison, Jr., was busy touting *his* plan for a 133-million-dollar subway system to replace the Union Loop. His was yet another in a seemingly endless series of such proposals put forward over the years and all of which, in one way or another, could be traced back to the original Bion Arnold recommendations of 1902. In 1916, the Traction and Subway Committee of the City Council recommended that a mammoth subway system be built, to cost 275 million dollars. It would have included fifty-three miles of subway tunnels for the city's elevated lines, and five miles for an underground trolley tunnel. To gauge the magnitude and scope of this 1916 proposal, the Panama Canal (completed in 1914) bore a price tag of 352 million. Chicago was clearly "thinking big" about subways, and setting its sights on a big-league underground transit project.

Indeed, the city was gradually progressing beyond the "mere talk" stage. In 1926, fifteen honorable members of the City Council drew expense money from City Hall and journeyed by Pullman car to the east coast, there to inspect subways in Boston, New York and Philadelphia. Furthermore, there was a special fund accumulating to pay for proposed subway construction as decided. When, as the twentieth century got under way, a number of streetcar lines applied for extension of their franchises the resultant City Council ordinances required that the trolley companies begin paying into a so-called "traction fund" out of their profits, a fund that would be used for eventual subway construction. Still, nothing concrete happened until the administration of President Franklin D. Roosevelt made federal dollars available for public works projects. In 1937 the City of Chicago filed an application with the Works Progress Administration for a grant and loan. Both were approved.

Thus on Saturday, December 17, 1938, five months and a day after Samuel Insull died, Chicago broke ground for its first subway. At 2:15 in the afternoon, a motor caravan left City Hall with Mayor Edward J. Kelly and U.S. Public Works Administrator Harold L. Ickes aboard. At State Street just south of Chicago Avenue a speakers' platform had been set up, and before a gathering of three thousand persons the symbolic start was enacted. The crowd, in time-honored Chicago tradition, had been rousted out by local precinct captains, and the assortment of handmade banners and signs held aloft had as a common theme the heaping of praise upon the City Hall incumbent, Mayor Kelly. "This is Chicago's Christmas gift from Mayor Kelly," proclaimed one placard. Alderman Dorsey Crowe of the 42nd Ward was the master of ceremonies. One of the first speakers was Alderman Jim Quinn, chairman of the City Council's Committee on Local Transportation, a man who would go on to devote thirty-eight additional years of service to mass transit in Chicago.[11] The speechifying continued until, by the time Ickes was at last introduced, the crowd of party regulars was starting to feel the bite of the twenty-four degree cold, and was restive in anticipation of the several receptions planned for afterward. Ickes, undeterred by either temperature or the audience, proceeded to deliver a lengthy lecture on the role of public works in the great civilizations of the world, replete with lengthy quotations from classical Greek literature. Such educational oratory was not, to be sure, in the typical Chicago political style; when the ceremony finally ended, the refreshments were appreciated all the more, especially those that served to drive the December chill from the frozen party workers.

The subway that was begun in 1938 was not intended to be a replacement for the Union Loop, but rather a supplement to it. It was, however, clearly designed to divert passengers from the older facility. It called for two parallel north-south subways—one under State Street and the other a block to the west under Dearborn Street—which would allow some of the trains that fed the Loop to be routed underground. Once the two lines were complete, the sixty-eight peak-hour trains using the Loop were to be reduced to thirty-eight. Harking back to the 1913 through-routing plan which Insull instituted—and following a recommendation by Bion Arnold from as far back as 1911—the operating pattern for the new subway would permit through service between neighborhoods north and south of downtown Chicago. The South Side L and the successor to the Northwestern line would both run through the State Street subway. The Dearborn project would allow the original Metropolitan route to enter downtown from the northwest, rather than from the southwest. The Dearborn subway would, eventually, also allow the Logan Square branch of the old Metropolitan L to be through-routed with the Garfield service, which would decrease the number of train movements required to serve both lines.

Contrary to most subway construction hitherto completed in the United States, much the greater part of Chicago's tunnels were excavated by the "deep bore" construction method. Boston, New York and Philadelphia contractors relied largely on "shallow draft" tunneling, a procedure wherein a street first is excavated, then the subway tunnel built as a steel and concrete structure *in* the excavation, after which the thoroughfare gets rebuilt atop the tunnel. Deep-bore work was the style of tunneling prevalent in London, especially on the Yerkes-built tube lines, but previously used in this country chiefly for subaqueous work such as the Hudson Tubes. The deep-bore method, while more costly, involved less disruption of city streets. Less, but not none.

The State Street tunnel veered off the old Alley L right-of-way south of Roosevelt Road, within a short distance of the Loop; to be precise, just a mile and a half from the intersection of State and Madison, the spot which marks the focal point of Chicago. On the north side, the tunnel continued under State Street, and then Clybourn Avenue, for a greater distance before rejoining the old Northwestern L right-of-way at Armitage, three and a half miles from State and Madison. This additional tunnel construction was helpful in speeding up schedules, for the Northwestern had been built

Workmen install trackage in the Dearborn Street subway. (Author's collection)

with a number of time-consuming sharp curves between Armitage and the Loop. The new tunnel bypassed this restrictive routing.

On both the State Street and Dearborn Street lines soil and ground conditions dictated two different styles of deep-bore construction. Away from the heart of downtown—that is to say, north of the Chicago River on the State Street line and west of La Salle Street on the Dearborn subway—the soil is relatively firm, and a construction technique called "hand mining" was employed. Though workers had to operate inside a pressurized airlock, the tunnels could be excavated with hand-operated power tools, as in some methods of coal mining.

In the Loop area itself, the characteristic blue clay of Chicago was much "wetter" at subway depth, also there were more complex building foundations to contend with along the two routes. Here the tubes were put through using boring shields and pressurized air locks.[12]

Each subway consisted of two tunnels, one for trains in each direction. Each tunnel was built with its own boring shield, a hefty piece of equipment that was twenty-five feet in diameter and weighed 225 tons.

Two separate boring shields were thus used under State Street. They started their journey on the southern end of the proposed subway at 11th Street and burrowed northward to a point 280 feet south of the Chicago River. One shield started work in January, 1940, the second in March of the same year, and both completed their work in less than a year's time. This staggered start was deliberate; it allowed the second shield to do its work adjacent to a firm and stable tunnel built by the pace-setting first shield. (Similar staggered starts would also be made on the hand-mined sections of tunnel.) Twin shields were also used on the two tunnels of the Dearborn Street subway and they began their work at La Salle and Lake streets in March and April of 1940 respectively. Their course included a tricky 275-foot radius curve into Dearborn Street; nevertheless the work was completed by October of the year in which it began.

The two State Street shields were dismantled and taken out of the tubes; but the Dearborn project begun at this time was only the first phase of a larger effort. Consequently the shields were left in place for later use.

For "tunneling" across the Chicago River on the State Street line, a 200-foot long steel and concrete tube was built by the Graver Tank and Manufacturing Company in a South Chicago shipyard. It was floated out of its drydock in the fall of 1939 and towed up to the Loop, one puffing tugboat

A northbound CTA train in the State Street subway makes three separate stops as it moves along the world's longest railway platform.

pulling the huge floating structure while another kept it on a steady course from astern. The voyage took six hours. On December 13, 1939, the Merritt-Chapman and Scott Corporation, prime contractors on the river project, sank the prefabricated piece of transit right-of-way into a trench that had been dug by a clamshell dredge into the mud bottom of the Chicago River. Connections to the underground tubes were then made inside cofferdams built along the banks of the river.

A single contractor, the Healy Subway Construction Company, built the shield portions of both subways. Six different firms toiled on different portions of the hand-mined sections.

A unique feature of both the State and Dearborn subways was the installation of a single, extra-long platform to accomodate several station stops in the downtown area. Under State Street, a platform measuring a whopping 3300 feet extends from Lake Street all the way to Van Buren—the full longer dimension of the elevated Union Loop. Trains regularly

: Letter "A" in the destination sign indicates of two stopping patterns—"A" or "B"—train es in skip-stop territory. Alternate trains stop rnate stations, with several common stops at tations, thereby allowing a two track line to e faster speeds.

Above photo: With the world's tallest building—the Sears Tower—standing guard in the background, a train of Boeing-Vertol cars emerges from the Dearborn Street subway into the median strip right-of-way in the Congress Expressway.

make three separate stops along the giant platform, and it has garnered a listing in *The Guinness Book of World Records* as the longest underground railway platform in the world.[13] The Dearborn subway was also built with a three-stop platform, but it is shorter by 800 feet than its record-holding State Street cousin.

Wartime priorities forced a halt to work on the Dearborn Street subway when it was about three-quarters finished, but in October, 1943, the State Street subway was ready for business. The facility opened for revenue service after midnight on Sunday, October 17. A Ravenswood train left that line's Kimball Terminal north of downtown at 11:34 P.M. Saturday night with motorman William Mescher at the controls. It was bound for the Englewood branch on the South Side L and it entered the subway portal just south of Armitage Station at one and one-half minutes past midnight. Howard Street-to-Jackson Park trains were rerouted off the Loop L and into the new subway at the same hour.

CHAPTER NINE
A Subway Celebration

THE AFTERNOON PRECEDING THE INAUGURATION of formal revenue service in the State Street subway, Saturday the 16th, Chicago staged some noisy and colorful inaugural fanfare for its first subway line. Ten special CRT trains were dispatched out of a variety of terminals all over the sprawling elevated system and made their way to the two tunnel portals. The first of these to reach the subway and carry passengers beneath Chicago streets left Fullerton station at 9:15 A.M. The same Alderman Crowe who had presided at the ground-breaking in 1938 was the unofficial "skipper" of the train, although the actual motorman was a rapid transit veteran of thirty-two years by the name of Charles Bade. The first station the train reached inside the tunnel was North and Clybourn. Here the first of many ceremonies was held. The Lake View High School band did a spirited rendition of *El Capitan*, and while the mood was intended to be of joyful celebration, the ear-shattering sound of a brass band in a tile subway station was downright painful.

Between 10:25 and 10:45 the ten specials arrived at State and Madison. Once they unloaded and were in the clear, a red, white and blue ribbon was strung across the northbound track. At 10:47 A.M. Mayor Kelly wielded the ceremonial scissors and uttered these less than immortal words: "There we go." The mayor was also presented a polished subway control handle in honor of the event. He, in turn, gave it to Bernard J. Fallon, the man who was both trustee and executive officer of the financially troubled CRT and said: "It is now up to you to see that it is the best operated subway in the nation."

Thus, in the anxious year 1943—as the battle for Italy wore on—did Chicago join Boston, New York and Philadelphia as operators of big-time, downtown underground rapid transit networks.

The tube was then opened for citizen inspection, CRT officials went back to work to make ready for the midnight opening of the tunnel, and upstairs on State Street an hour-long parade marched to celebrate the event. Proclaimed Mayor Kelly: "This is the most significant event in Chicago history to date," in a rhetorical style that never seems to grow old in the city that is called windy.

The press was enthusiastic about the new subway. Describing the attitude aboard Alderman Crowe's special train on Saturday, a *Tribune* reporter wrote that "sophisticated Chicagoans got boy-like thrills" when the elevated train descended the incline and became a subway train. A Sunday supplement on inaugural weekend called the effort "the most glorified hole in the ground that has ever been designed," and did not fail to carry on the Chicago tradition of comparing the tunnel—favorably, of course—to its New York precedessors. While the *Chicago Tribune* lavished much editorial comment on the new subway during its years of construction, on the day the tube finally opened the editorial page was silent on transit matters. Instead it directed attention to another issue then causing some concern: "Never Again a Third Term."

The Chicago subway had an Art Deco "look" that was popular during the WPA era, and it also marked the very first use of fluorescent lighting in subway stations. But while some Chicago commentators felt that the State Street line was superior to subways in New York in appointments and design, its outfitting was downright Spartan in comparison to what had by then become typical New York subway architecture. In the stations with center platforms, the side walls flanking the tracks were left in unfinished concrete. In New York, such a station would include fully tiled walls. So, while there was nothing at all untasteful about the State Street subway, it could hardly be called artistically distinguished. Functional, yes; artistic, no.

The State Street subway measured 4.9 miles portal to portal. At each entry point trackage had been realigned so that trains bound for the new subway descended a grade in the middle of the elevated structure. As much as possible, old steel from the original L alignment was used to build the

Action at the junction where the State Street subway joins the old Soute Side L. Train of 6000 series cars heads northbound into the subway, while a 95th Street-bound Lake Dan-Ryan rumbles past on the L.

Light at the end of the tunnel. A southbound train has completed its trip through the State Street subway and emerges into daylight to continue its run to Jackson Park.

subway ramps; those wartime scarcities made new girders difficult to come by! At both portal locations, the older overhead route into the Union Loop was retained and train schedules developed that took advantage of this overhead or underground flexibility in routing.

The cost of the project was heavy. Together the State and Dearborn tubes bore a price tag of 64 million dollars. Of this sum, 23 million was federal public works assistance, and slightly over 40 million dollars was provided by the City of Chicago's traction fund, the money that had accumulated over the years from the franchise fees exacted from the surface lines. The statutes under which the Chicago subways were built resulted in some seemingly arbitrary distinctions. The Chicago Rapid Transit Company would run its trains through the city-owned tunnels; therefore, the traction company was expected to finance the cost of track and signals. In reality, CRT was so fiscally anemic that conventional financing for such capital investments was out of the question. The company had to obtain a special purpose loan from the city, and would barely survive at all until war's end.

CHAPTER TEN
Enter the CTA

By 1943 it had become apparent that further private-owner operation of public mass transportation services in the City of Chicago could not continue. Very much in the wind in the early 1940s was the complete unification of all mass transit under public auspices: elevated trains, streetcars, buses, and now even subway operations.

As we have seen, this was not exactly a novel idea in Chicago. After the departure of Charles Tyson Yerkes, enough agitation developed for public ownership and operation of Chicago mass transit to bring about a referendum on the matter. On April 1, 1902, Chicago voters expressed their opinion in favor of public ownership by a count of 142,826 to 27,998. The Insull era, of course, did bring something of a reprieve for private ownership, at least insofar as the elevated lines were concerned. After the collapse of Insull's empire, there could be no further way to hide the hopeless financial plight of the CRT.

On Wednesday before the gala opening of the State Street subway, Mayor Kelly submitted a plan for transit unification to the City Council. This was not a pivotal development in itself, but it did serve as a barometer of how policy was developing. Many more reports, studies and proposals were necessary before public ownership would come to pass. In April, 1945, just days before World War II was to end in Europe, the Illinois state legislature passed an act which created a public transit authority for metropolitan Chicago. Many elevated lines, of course, extended beyond the Chicago city limits and served suburban communities in Cook County; hence the new agency would have a jurisdiction that crossed municipal boundries. On June 4, 1945, the matter was put to public referendum and it passed by a margin of six to one. Much pulling and hauling was still necessary to arrange the orderly transfer of assets from private to public hands, and it was not until October 1, 1947, that the Chicago Transit Authority—abbreviated CTA—took over the operations of both the Chicago Rapid Transit Company and the Chicago Surface Lines, the latter being the single company that had evolved as the operator of streetcars in the Windy City.[14] A bond issue in the amount of 105 million dollars was floated to fund the transfer, twelve million dollars being the negotiated price for the assets and good name of the CRT and seventy-five million dollars required for Chicago Surface Lines to meld into the public sector. The rest of the money was used for immediate capital improvements to the two deteriorated systems.

Chicago Surface Lines, incidently, was the largest single operator of streetcars in the entire United States. This status it managed to achieve because in the City of New York a number of different companies operated trolley cars, even though, collectively, Gotham had more streetcars than Chicago. There would later be a third major private company absorbed into the CTA. The Chicago Motor Coach Co. came to the end of its corporate tether in 1952 when its routes and assets became part of the CTA.

The CTA was put under the charge of a board of directors, a group named the Chicago Transit Board, which began holding regular meetings in 1945.[15] There's a story told about the early days which may well be apocryphal, but bears repeating. It seems the enabling legislation for the new transit authority did not positively state that it be called "The Chicago Transit Authority," but merely authorized the creation of a "a metropolitan transit authority." Years later this oversight was discovered by a zealous legal type, or so goes the story, and corrective legislation had to be quietly passed to sanction, retroactively, the use of the proper name on such legal instruments as labor contracts and real estate deeds. Bureaucracy knows no bounds!

Also, on the matter of the CTA's once and future name, it should be noted that the celebrated rock music group "Chicago" first burst on the scene with a somewhat longer title. The group called itself "The Chicago Transit Authority" in its early days, but opted for the shorter title when the real CTA took exception to the usage.

Service on the Dearborn Street subway had to wait for the lifting of wartime restrictions. Here's Washington Street station in 1978, twenty-seven years after the opening, hosting a train of Boeing-Vertol 2400 series cars.

Thus it was, when the Dearborn Street subway was eventually opened after wartime restrictions were lifted, that the new CTA operated the route. (The City of Chicago had resumed work on the project in late 1945 when it advertised for bids to build the hand-mined western portion of the route.)

The first revenue train to ply the new tunnel left Logan Square terminal at 12:01 A.M. on February 25, 1951, and dipped into the new tube four minutes later. A motorman named Wallace Hurford handled the controls. Although the downtown Dearborn Street subway was designed to connect with older elevated lines at each of its two ends, just like the State Street line, when operations commenced in 1951 it was fed only from one end, the northwest. For seven years thereafter trains using the new facility terminated at the La Salle Street station, near those still-in-place tunnel shields used in building the tube back before the war. L trains inbound from Logan

Above, left: That's Tower 18; the date is August 16, 1950, and the action in the foreground is the inaugural run of new 6000 series cars. (George Krambles Collection)

Square left the elevated alignment after departing from the Damen Avenue station and via an incline into the new tunnel. Then, instead of following the original circuitous Metropolitan West Side route into the Loop from the southwest, the new subway continued on a direct course under Milwaukee Avenue to Lake Street at the Chicago River. At the point where the twin tunnels, curve from Milwaukee into Lake Street, and tunnel under the Lake Street L, they are built at separate grades. The reason for this? Should the Lake Street L ever be tied into the Dearborn subway, the connection could be made without disturbing the older tunnel. Tunnel headings do exist at Lake and Milwaukee that indeed may someday become part of a Lake Street subway.[16]

Unlike the State Street project, where the older elevated hookups with the Loop were retained, the elevated between the Loop and the line to Logan Square was eventually torn down. Though it remained in place for a few years after the Dearborn subway opened, it was only used for shop moves.

Mayor Martin H. Kennelly presided at a ribbon-cutting ceremony at Madison and Dearborn on opening day, Saturday, February 25th. "It's a great day for Chicago and particularly the northwest side," suggested His Honor. Participating with the mayor at the ceremony was radio and cinema personality Monte Blue, decked out in his usual cowboy costume. To emphasize how the new line would save time for commuting northwest residents by virtue of the elimination of the Metropolitan's old roundabout route to the Loop, CTA invested in paid newspaper advertising to call patrons' attention to the new service. Illustrating the ads were photographs of the CTA's equally new subway and L vehicles.

Chicago's Celebrated 6000 Series Cars

In 1947, when CTA took over the elevated lines, the condition of the line's transit equipment was, in a word, deplorable—visible evidence of the financial ill health of the Chicago Rapid Transit Company. Except for a quartet of experimental three-section articulated units ordered by CRT immediately after World War II, the most recent passenger cars on what had at last become, and remains, the nation's second largest rapid transit system were twenty years old.[17] Only 455 of the CTA's total car roster of approximately 1,200 units were of all-steel construction. These were cars designed and built during the early days of the Insull era, and had it not been for the capital which Insull provided, it is anyone's guess how the fleet might have survived the traffic demands of World War II. By law, only all-steel cars could run in the subways, for instance, and the lack of new rolling stock was a major embarrassment when the State Street subway opened in 1943. A souvenir booklet prepared by the City of Chicago for the occasion contained many photographs of the new stations, but none with trains in evidence. In the back of the booklet, a picture was included of a new, experimental train built for the New York system in 1940 by the Clark Railway Equipment Corporation. "New cars must await unification of the local transit companies or the availability of cash from other sources," read the apologetic caption. The steel cars built during the Insull regime were nothing to be ashamed of, but when the State Street subway opened, the newest of the lot was twenty years old. The city fathers felt their new tunnel deserved better.

For the remainder of its L services, in order to fulfill daily assignments, the CTA perforce had to rely on a roster of hand-me-down equipment that dated back to the original four L companies. Cars that once ran on the Alley L at the turn of the century were still in regular service, and a plethora of

rebuildings and renovations committed over the years on one or another class of these cars, all combined to saddle the CTA with a most inefficient and unwieldly—although admittedly quite picturesque—fleet. Many L vehicles originally built as open-platform cars, with hand-operated gates to control passenger entry and exit, had been reoutfitted with enclosed vestibules and sliding doors so that appearances belied their age. Clearly a major and urgent replacement program had to be the fledgling public authority's first priority. And so it was!

The resulting cars have been known throughout their years of service as the "6000 series." Moreover they have become identified as *the* Chicago rapid transit car, a distinction eminently justified on numerous counts. They have made cameo appearances in several Hollywood films that have utilized a Chicago location, and for many years television's "Bob Newhart Show" used footage of the 6000 series cars at the start of each week's episode to establish the location as being Chicago and nowhere else. A cultural impact indeed, but still more important is the fact that the 6000 series incorporated some design features for rapid transit equipment that just as eloquently proclaim the fleet "Chicago" as does the CTA identification logo blazoned on each unit.

Incorporating several design innovations which were pioneered on the four experimental articulated units, the new cars were greatly influenced by

Left: Six-car train on the Wabash leg of the Loop. Originally, the 6000 series cars looked like this: twin headlamps down low, destination sign over the door. Before the order was completed, CTA changed the specification, placing the destination sign inside the left front window and substituting a single sealed-beam headlight over the door. Most of the earlier cars were converted to the new specification, yet as late as 1977 one could occasionally find an example of the original look.

THE "BLINKER"DOORS

Alone among U.S. rapid transit systems, CTA featured "trolley-car style," or "blinker," doors. These distinguished not only the 6000 series cars but the post-war articulated units, the Pullman-Standard (2000 series) and the original Budd cars (2200 series). With the advent of the Boeing-Vertol vehicles and the new stainless steel Budd 2600 series, there was a reversion to the conventional transit style of sliding door (last seen in Chicago on the Insull-ero 4000 series) largely to accommodate wheelchairs, a Federal-funding stipulation for the convenience of the handicapped.

In the station scene at right, we see a blinker-door entrance in the open position, as a final rider crowds aboard under the watchful eye of a guard.

Below: November 8, 1950. New 6000 series cars were operating on the Logan Square-Union Loop line, just days before this service was re-routed. View is at Randolph/Wells. (George Krambles Collection)

the highly successful "PCC type" of streetcar that had become the standard vehicle of the industry following its introduction in 1936. In a breakaway from conventional rapid transit practice elsewhere in North America, units of the 6000 fleet designed by CTA were not equipped with air brakes, but instead were equipped with a mechanical-electrical braking system, making it possible to do away with all the cumbersome apparatus of an air system—compressors, air tanks, train lines. The absence of "air" on the CTA cars greatly simplifies the process of putting a train into service from a storage yard. A motorman does not have to wait for air pressure to pump up to operable levels; no longer can condensation freeze up on sub-zero mornings (as in a braking system that requires an air line). All that's necessary is to throw a switch and feed power to the motors. CTA claims, too, that on those few occasions when fire threatens a storage yard full of trains, equipment can be quickly moved out of harm's way, thanks to the instant response mobility of the 6000 series cars.[18]

Other design influences stemmed from the severe clearance "envelope" bequeathed to CTA by its predecessors. On the elevated systems curves were very sharp and the platforms had been constructed to accomodate transit equipment that measured a little shy of nine feet in width. There were many other transit systems in the United States built to *roughly* similar specification, notably the Interborough Rapid Transit (IRT) and the

A two-car train of 6000 series cars moves clockwise along the Lake Street leg of the Loop. This was the midday Loop Shuttle service, a since discontinued operation.

State Street subway; 6000 series cars.

Hudson & Manhattan (Hudson Tubes) in New York, the Market Street line in Philadelphia, and elements of the Boston system. But later construction, such as the Broad Street subway in Philadelphia, the Cambridge line in Boston, and the rest of the New York system accommodated subway cars fully ten feet wide and up to seventy feet in length, with appropriate curvature for handling such equipment. Of course, the price paid for these generous dimensions was subway systems composed of incompatible elements, the newer and larger cars forever barred from operating on the constricted older routes.

However, the Chicago Transit Authority was committed to operating a single, unified rapid transit system; its brand new rolling stock must perforce be designed with respect to clearances established before the turn of the century. To squeeze a little more usable room into each unit the 6000 cars' sidewalls cant outward above floor level. Thus the 6000s would observe platform clearances on the elevated system, yet the new equipment was wider than previous stock. The 6000 series cars were also quite light in weight. A typical CTA steel car weighed over seventy-five thousand pounds; the newcomers scaled in at just under sixty thousand pounds. Whereas older equipment had two motors in the 150 h.p. range mounted both on a single truck; the 6000 series was powered by 55 h.p. motors, two on each truck, providing acceleration markedly swifter than that of the older vehicles.

Out of what would eventually be a fleet of 770 similar cars, all but fifty were built as permanently-coupled two-car sets—"married pairs," as they are often called in the transit industry—with but a single motorman's cab per car. The odd fifty were built as single unit double-ended cars equipped with a motorman's cab at each end. These cars were not even numbered in the 6000 series, and some purists would insist they should be regarded as quite separate from the basic fleet, which they would reduce in number to 720 units. The single-unit cars, which are virtually "look-alikes" of authentic 6000 series vehicles, were carried on the roster as Nos. 1 through 50. Over the years several of these cars have been outfitted with various custom-built and/or experimental components of one sort or another.

CTA's first order for 130 units, at a cost of $36,000 each, was placed with the St. Louis Car Company on September 1, 1948. Deliveries began in the summer of 1950 and the cars drew exceptionally laudatory comments in the press. These were the cars that opened the Dearborn Street subway in February, 1951. Subsequently, additional orders were placed, all with St. Louis, until the fifty single units and the last twenty-five "married pairs" were delivered in 1959. Over the decade during which they were built, costs increased to $63,000 per car, an escalation of seventy-five percent. As the new 6000 series fleet grew, of course, CTA was able to phase out its older wooden equipment—generally referred to in press releases as "wood-steel" cars to reassure passengers that they were not being forced to ride in frontier-era equipment. Such "wooden" cars had steel underframes and, often, metal bodyframing as well. The last such cars to haul revenue passengers in Chicago did so on December 1, 1957.

CTA also managed to cut back its overall rapid transit car roster during the 1950s. During the previous quarter-century, the system fleet numbered some 1,700 units. Following the introduction of the 6000 series cars the roster was reduced to a 1,200-car, more or less, range. The 6000s had only marginally greater passenger capacity than their wood-steel predecessors, since both types were forced to respect the same clearances. The new equipment was more reliable, of course, and thus some number of "spares" could be eliminated from the total roster. Likewise the 6000s could handle a given service with fewer cars because their improved acceleration moved traffic along more swiftly, especially if an entire route could be equipped exclusively with the new vehicles. Yet the single most important factor that allowed CTA to reduce its car fleet by almost thirty percent was the outright elimination of many lightly-trafficked outlying branch lines of the elevated system. These were built during the days of open competition between streetcars and the L companies. Now unified CTA could reduce such excess mileage, and redeploy its surface lines as feeders to a trimmed-down trunk-line rail system.

Something of a novelty in the construction of the 6000 series cars was the

use of "traded in" trolley cars in their manufacture. This arrangement has often been misunderstood. The CTA 6000 series cars are not, in any sense, "rebuilt" streetcars. What took place was the sequel to a purchase, by the City of Chicago, of 600 new PCC-type trolley cars immediately after VJ Day, for what was then still a privately owned and operated surface-line company, but one which (as things turned out) was well on the way to becoming part of a unified and publicly owned transit system. The transaction was consummated on the mistaken assumption that such equipment would have its place in the post-war scheme of things. Registrations of private automobiles in Chicago—which first hit the half-million mark in 1937 and remained within a hundred thousand of that figure throughout the war years—started to rise as soon as automobile manufacturing resumed, along with the conversion of streetcar to motorbus lines. Chicago, anxious to do this but still recoup as much as possible from the city's hasty post-war investment in new trolley cars, developed a deal with St. Louis Car Company.

Five hundred sixty of the practically brand-new streetcars would, in essence, be scrapped. But trucks, motors, window sash, mechanical equipment—any usable components—would be salvaged and utilized in the subsequent construction of the otherwise all-new cars for subways and Ls.

Governmental procurement dealings in America are often stigmatized, correctly or otherwise, as inefficient, wasteful and bumbling. Chicago's acquisition of the 6000 series rapid transit cars by and for the CTA must be characterized as a truly smart and pragmatic accomplishment.

Two single-unit cars assigned to the Skokie Swift pause at the CTA's Howard Street Terminal, where they connect with the main north-south trunk line of the transit system. Note streetcar style folding doors, also the overhead power collection gear for use on the ex-North Shore route.

On the Northwestern L, circa 1954. Charles Tyson Yerkes built this four-track elevated line, and it remains one of Chicago's busiest. On the center tracks, express trains to and from the State Street subway pass at speed. On the outside tracks, two locals are operating between the Ravenswood branch and the Union Loop. Venerable "wood-steel" train on the left is seeing its final days as the last units of 6000 series cars will soon arrive on the property. (Author's collection)

CTA's north-south trunk line operates through the State Street subway and terminates at Howard Street, almost ten miles north of State and Madison. One of the system's nine storage and repair yards is off to the right, and two branch lines continue beyond this point into suburban residential communities. Tracks of the Evanston Branch proceed directly away from the photographer in the center, while the ex-North Shore line that is today CTA's Skokie Swift bends off to the left. A four-car train of 6000 series cars is entering the Howard Street station, bound for downtown Chicago, in this 1973 scene.

CHAPTER ELEVEN
CTA Expansion

THE DEARBORN STREET SUBWAY, as opened for business in 1951, was incomplete, a fragment of a subway. Its trains utilized the new tube from Logan Square, but the route chopped off in dead-end fashion, so to speak, at the La Salle Street station under and behind the railroad terminal of the same name. Plans had always called for bringing this subway out of the Loop area at its southwest quadrant, to tie it into the Garfield line of the Metropolitan West Side system. The Garfield L itself did not, however, survive. It was torn down after World War II, to be replaced by a new and different kind of rapid transit line, a ground-level right-of-way built into the median strip of the new Congress Expressway.[19] In this manner, then, was the Dearborn Street subway connected up, despite original plans, with the new Congress line westward. At last the Metropolitan's original Van Buren and Wells southwest corner entry onto the Union Loop could be dismantled. Interestingly, during construction of the Congress Expressway a unique, temporary rerouting of Garfield L trains into the Loop was effected—the "temporary" lasting for three years, right up to the opening of the subway link-up with the Congress line in 1958. As did all four elevated companies, the Metropolitan had a stub-end terminal near the Loop that could be used by those excess rush-hour trains the Loop itself could not accommodate. The Metropolitan's terminal was on Wells Street. The four stub-end tracks in the terminal came in from the west at an angle perpendicular to the Wells Street leg of the Union Loop, and at the same elevated grade above street level. (See map, page 42).

This rerouting, however necessary, involved the CTA in a pesky demolition-construction project. The Metropolitan's terminal building itself stood between tracks' end and the Wells Street segment of the Loop. Not only must CTA tear this barrier down but afterward build a replacement viaduct so that the erstwhile stub-end terminal tracks could serve as an entry onto the Loop elevated.

Yet this was hardly the most troublesome or unusual problem to be overcome as work on the Dearborn Street subway moved toward completion. Standing smack in the path of the subway tunnel as it progressed westward from La Salle Street was the seemingly impenetrable bulk of Chicago's main post office. (The Congress Expressway actually goes *through* this building.) Subway construction work crews, *very* carefully, had to extract sixteen foundation caissons of the massive structure, toiling within a pressurized air lock below street level. Then, subsequent to the construction of the twin subway tunnels, those caissons had to be replaced around and in some cases on top of the newly built transit tubes. The CTA tunnel, in effect, now contributes to the support of the post office.

Once the Dearborn Street subway and its link-up with the Congress line was finished, all of the ex-Metropolitan service ceased operation on the Loop. In 1949 such residual trains of the old South Side L that were still running onto the Union Loop were rerouted into the State Street subway. The only remaining trains using the Alley L's entry onto the Loop were interurbans of the Chicago, North Shore & Milwaukee Railroad, a privately operated service that reached downtown Chicago over CRT/CTA trackage.[20] When this line was abandoned outright in 1963, there seemed to be no future for the elevated link-up with the South Side line; the only trains now using the Union Loop entered and departed the facility at Lake and Wells, the interlocking controlled by enduring old Tower 18. Indeed with the advent of the two downtown subways, the stub-end terminals of each of the four elevated lines (located from the beginning just outside the Loop) were phased out of service.[21] The Loop was still busily engaged, of course, but its service pattern had changed.

CHAPTER TWELVE
More Loop Service

THE LOOP WAS TO SEE SOMETHING of a renaissance in 1969. Thanks to the availability of capital assistance grants from the United States Department of Transportation, Chicago built two new rapid transit lines—both in the median strips of new expressways, a style of construction pioneered on the Congress line in 1958. The Kennedy line is an extension of the old Metropolitan service that had long terminated at Logan Square. Now, running beyond Logan Square in a short two-station subway, the line emerges in the median strip of the Kennedy Expressway. It opened on February 1, 1970 as far as the Jefferson Park terminal, a convenient interchange point between the new transit line, CTA and suburban feeder buses, the Chicago & North Western Railroad's commuter line to Crystal Lake, and Greyhound bus service to places as far distant as Seattle. (Work began in 1979 to build this line an additional six miles to O'Hare International Airport, thus enabling CTA passengers to transfer to vehicles heading for Shannon, Frankfurt, London and Tokyo.)

South of the Loop runs the multi-lane Dan Ryan Expressway, and a new rapid transit line in the median strip of this roadway opened for revenue service on September 28, 1969. The new line has its southern terminal at 95th Street and the Dan Ryan Expressway, the southernmost point on the CTA rapid transit system. Heading north to the Loop, the transit line leaves the expressway alignment at 18th Street and joins the old South Side right-of-way a mere hundred or so yards from the point where the South Side line has its entry into the State Street subway. The new Dan Ryan line then proceeds onto the Union Loop over the very same Alley L right-of-way that was first traveled by snorting steam L trains on the June morning in 1892 when so many people thought James G. Blaine would beat out incumbent Benjamin Harrison for the GOP presidential nomination.

CTA linked up the new Dan Ryan line with the Lake Street L in a through-routing arrangement. As before, in the initial inauguration of through-routing in 1913, major revisions in Loop operating practice were necessary. This time the Loop was turned into a conventional, two-way operation on all its legs. The two-way operation instituted in 1969, however, differed from that in use between 1897 and 1913 in that it was—and remains—a "right hand" service. Trains on the outside Loop track now operate counterclockwise, and trains on the inside Loop track operate clockwise.[22]

Tower 18 Is Dead! Long Live Tower 18!

The Loop service revisions of 1969 made old Tower 18 a casualty of progress. The tower, as built, was situated smack in the middle of the Wells-Lake intersection, a location also right in the path Lake Street trains must follow in the new alignment. A modern Tower 18 was perforce erected clear of the right-of-way and the old two-story frame structure—which at one time was considered to be the busiest railway tower in the entire world—was phased out of service on Sunday, September 6, 1969, and soon thereafter dismantled. The original structure dated back to the opening of the Union Loop in 1897 and was at that time equipped with a hand-operated lever form of switch and signal control. In 1907 this was retired in favor of an electro-pneumatic interlocking system which survived until 1969, although it was extensively re-rigged at the time of the 1913 through-routing. The present-day Tower 18 is a busy, even a frantic spot, especially during rush hours. One of the most soul-stirring experiences in all of U.S. rapid transit is to see—and *hear*—an eight-car Lake-Dan Ryan train hammer across the diamond at speed and with no hesitation. Still it's nothing like it used to be in the days before the subways were built when the L crews manning Tower 18 would be called upon to make hundreds of split-second decisions all day long. The built-in safety of the 1907

A CTA operator mans the interlocking machine in one of the many control towers along the sprawling elevated system. (Author's collection)

interlocking system was a help, for it meant that an incorrectly set switch could not result in a collision. But it was perfectly possible for a towerman to make a wrong guess, or two, and wind up delaying the entire railroad. Let's listen in: . . . . *set the signals for a southbound Ravenswood, and leave a red board for an eastbound Lake, because the train ahead on the track where the Ravenswood goes seems ready to move along. But he doesn't, and the Ravenswood has to stop before its last car clears the interlock, and now the entire intersection is blocked. And just when it looks like everybody's about to start moving again, the telephone rings. It's the Wells Street bridge saying they're going to raise the span to let a coal barge through. That means there's no place to put eight Northwestern trains making their way around the Loop when they get back to Tower 18 because the about-to-be-opened Wells Street bridge is the only link between the Northwestern L and the Loop. . . .*

Lake-Dan Ryan traffic now uses Lake Street and Wabash Avenue in both directions; this service never ventures over the Van Buren or Wells segments of the Loop. Ravenswood trains from the old Northwestern

Action at Tower 18, in its new configuration and position, during midday at Lake and Wells. On the scene are two "married pairs" of 2000 series Pullman-built cars in Bicentennial livery. Near train is inbound from Oak Park on the Lake Street route; far train has come up from 95th Street on the Dan Ryan line. (CTA)

system enter the Loop at Lake and Wells and execute a counter-clockwise circuit over the outside track. Evanston Express service, more or less a rush-hour-only operation, makes a clockwise run on the inside rails. A Loop shuttle service that ran continuously over the inside track was inaugurated at the time of the 1969 change-over, but quietly dropped in 1977 as an economy move.

Throughout its entire life, the two-mile, double-tracked elevated line that circuits the business district of the nation's second largest city has coexisted with strong pressures, political and civic, to do away with it in favor of a subway. Today, the venerable Loop is the last such overhead rapid transit line to serve the downtown area of *any* U.S. city. Downtown els in both Manhattan and Brooklyn have been replaced with subways. In Philadelphia and Boston, where the elevated lines never really were built into the heart of central business districts, elevated mileage has nonetheless been reduced by the construction of new subways, so that the els are more than ever farther away from the downtown areas.

The Union Loop in Chicago remains virtually and placidly what it has been since its early days. Trackage has been reworked to accommodate changing operational modes, and a new electronic signal system, as advanced as any in the world, is now in place.[23] Stations have been added, lengthened, consolidated and eliminated in response to changing riding habits. Save for an effort at Wabash and Randolph where a totally new waiting room was built in the 1960s, and except for the installation of a few escalators between street and platform levels, the facility is little different, in any major respect, for today's passenger from what it was for a passenger at the turn of the century. The same support columns which drew such ire when the Loop opened in 1897 play havoc with today's traffic, too. The only accomodation to criticism has been the removal, from time to time, of a few especially obstructive support members at various cross streets.

Something of an irony, and one that gives some support to those who claim that bygone workmanship is superior to anything contemporary, happened in early 1978 when service between the Loop and the Dan Ryan line had to be suspended temporarily because of cracked girders in the connecting link between the Loop and the lately built median-strip transit line. The flaws were detected quite accidentally by a passenger on a Rock Island Railroad commuter train. He happened to be an engineer and he also happened one day to glance up while passing under the CTA elevated line. But it was not the old Alley L structure of 1892 that gave way; it was the new elevated segment built for the Dan Ryan line in 1969![24]

CHAPTER THIRTEEN

Today's Equipment

If the Loop elevated structure remains largely unchanged, transit rolling stock is an area that has seen steady improvement since Labor Day in 1897, when motor unit No. 101 of the Lake Street L made the very first trip around the Union Loop. Car No. 101 was built by Pullman in 1894 as a wooden trailer coach for use behind the L company's steam locomotives. The year after it was built, the McGuire Company of Chicago outfitted No. 101 with the two General Electric No. 55 traction motors as a step in the Chicago L's changeover to the new energy form. On October 6, 1976, the Chicago Loop saw yet another phase in the long evolutionary sequence of transit car design when a four-car test train of spanking new air-conditioned, stainless steel rapid transit cars were taken out for their inaugural trip. The run was exclusively for VIPs and the press and involved a turn over the Loop, down the Dan Ryan line, and back for a luncheon celebration at the Merchandise Mart. Mayor Richard J. Daley was aboard. It turned out to be his last ride on a CTA train; he died that December.

The new cars were constructed for the CTA by the Boeing-Vertol Company, the helicopter-building arm of a firm whose major product is passenger jetliners. Following delivery of the first units of the two hundred cars ordered, the CTA began the systematic retirement of the 6000 series cars. In 1978 contracts were signed with the Budd Company for what eventually became an order for six hundred additional cars of a similar design. Arrival of these cars will enable CTA to retire virtually all the 6000 series, and thus equip the system with a fleet that will be only a few units short of being totally air-conditioned. With typical Chicago straightforwardness, the new stainless steel cars were dubbed the "2600 series" at the time the first units, bearing the numbers 2601 and 2602, arrived from Budd's Philadelphia works in 1981. However, because there are hundreds more cars to come, it remains to be seen whether the original name will stick with the fleet throughout its entire service life.

It should not, of course, be assumed that CTA was inactive in equipment procurement during the interval between the arrival of the last 6000 series car in 1959 and the purchase of the Boeing units in 1976. There were two major orders placed and delivered: 180 cars from Pullman-Standard in 1964 and 150 cars from Budd in 1969–70. These 330 units could not operate in trains with the 6000 series cars, but could, and do, intermix with each other and with the even newer Boeing and Budd products. Together they represent an appropriate improvement over the 6000 series fleet, an advance that passengers can readily appreciate on the hot summer days Chicago seems to have so many of—air-conditioning. However, in line with CTA's passion for dependable, simplified car design, they retain the 6000 series' braking system and there is no indulgence in some of the more exotic electronic hardware that has appeared on newer rapid transit systems around the country.

The arrival of the Budd cars in 1970 provided CTA with sufficient equipment to have retired the last of the steel cars that dated to the Insull era, but these old-timers managed a reprieve for a few years. Many were equipped with roof-mounted trolley poles, as well as conventional third-rail shoes, for current collection. In bygone years, several CRT/CTA routes drew power from overhead trolley wire in outlying areas where trains ran on ground-level right-of-way; perforce large numbers of cars had been rigged to draw current from either system. The Evanston line on the old

Northwestern system was the last of such CTA overhead trolley routes.[25] Because very few of the 6000 series cars were ever equipped with trolley poles, it was a small fleet of 4000 series cars from the 1920s that continued to run in Evanston service up to November, 1973, when a third rail was installed on the Evanston line and the 4000s were retired.

The 1969–70 Budd cars are unpainted stainless steel vehicles, whereas the 1964 Pullman cars require a coating of protective enamel. As delivered they were liveried in green and white to match what was planned to be the new color scheme for the 6000 series cars. After the Budd cars arrived, however, CTA worked out a very attractive gun-metal and gray color scheme for the Pullman cars. This goes so well with the stainless steel units that a mix of Budd and Pullman products causes no visual distraction.

On the subject of color schemes, it should be noted that with but a single major and several minor exceptions, the CTA has had but two livery designs for the 6000 series cars. As delivered, the vehicles were done up in a three-color rendition which the uninitiated might be tempted to call green and cream with an orange stripe. Pity the uninitiated! The official, authentic, not-to-be-trifled-with specification for CTA rapid transit cars—and PCC streetcars likewise—called for these hues: Mercury green and Croydon cream, with Swamp Holly orange for trim! For that matter, a simpler green-and-white scheme introduced in 1965 did not suffer for lack of distinctive nomenclature. Though not quite in the same exalted, colorful

At the Oak Park terminal of the Lake Street L—today referred to as Lake-Dan Ryan service—a 2000 series Pullman-built car awaits departure time.

Boeing debut. On October 6, 1976, CTA cars Nos. 2401 through 2404 were unveiled for the press and Chicago VIPs, shown here at the Merchandise Mart station of the old Northwestern L after completing an inaugural trip to 95th Street on the Dan Ryan line and back. The 200-car order was built by the helicopter-building arm of the giant Boeing Company. (Boeing-Vertol)

Latest rolling stock on the CTA is a fleet of six hundred Budd-built cars such as No. 2602, shown here at Skokie Shops. Like the Boeing-Vertol cars, the Budd cars feature traditional rapid transit sliding doors. (CTA)

CRT lives! One of the four experimental articulated units built for Chicago Rapid Transit at the end of World War II shows off its new American Revolutionary Bicentennial livery along third rail trackage of the Skokie Swift in 1975. The four units survive in rush hour service on the Swift because they can be operated by a single crew member. (CTA photo)

Left: Interior view: CTA articulated unit No. '75, "Paul Revere." (CTA)

Below: CTA's first set of cars to be decorated in patriotic livery for the American Revolutionary Bicentennial was this pair of 2000 series Pullman cars. Not only were the pair christened "Ben Franklin" but they were renumbered 1775 and 1776. (CTA)

league as "Swamp Holly orange," to be sure, this second color adornment for the 6000 series was: Mint green and Alpine white.

There were minor but extensive exceptions to these two liveries, which took the form of experimental and/or one-time patterns that emerged from time to time. The major exception was a Bicentennial Year effort to decorate a representative sample of cars and buses in red, white and blue. Most of such units were also assigned names with Revolutionary War connotation. Conjunctively, CTA's public relations office cranked out a series of press releases that almost constitute a high-school textbook on the War for Independence. Such lesser known patriots as Haym Salomon (car Nos. 6017–18) and Charles Wilson Peale (car Nos. 6505–06) joined the likes of Patrick Henry (car Nos. 6473–74) and George Washington (car Nos. 6711–12) and more than a dozen others in a rolling tribute to the "Spirit of '76." CTA's latest rolling stock, from both Boeing-Vertol and Budd, has arrived from the factory decked out in a somewhat restrained version of this patriotism in color.

CHAPTER FOURTEEN
End of the Loop?

IN 1970 THE CHICAGO CITY COUNCIL created an entity called the Chicago Urban Transit District, inevitably referred to as C.U.T.D. This public body was mandated to design and build a subway replacement for the elevated Loop. C.U.T.D. was also empowered to levy taxes within its service district for funds which might become the seed money for massive Federal assistance, at last, to inter the venerable Union Loop. Meetings took place, consultants were hired, plans drawn up, operational schemes simulated on computers. But C.U.T.D. quickly ran up against one unavoidable and irreducible fact. The Union Loop that cost less than a million dollars to build in 1897 will require, perhaps, two billion or more dollars to replace at today's construction prices. Quickly an earlier plan to build sufficient downtown subways to duplicate the Loop's particular distribution pattern was scaled down to more modest levels. First, a new north-south tube under Franklin Street would be constructed so that Ravenswood and Evanston trains from the north could be through-routed southward over the Dan Ryan line and, thusly, removed from the elevated Loop. This would leave the Lake Street service still using the Loop—or some portion of it—perhaps in a manner reminiscent of the late summer of 1897 when the Loop was being

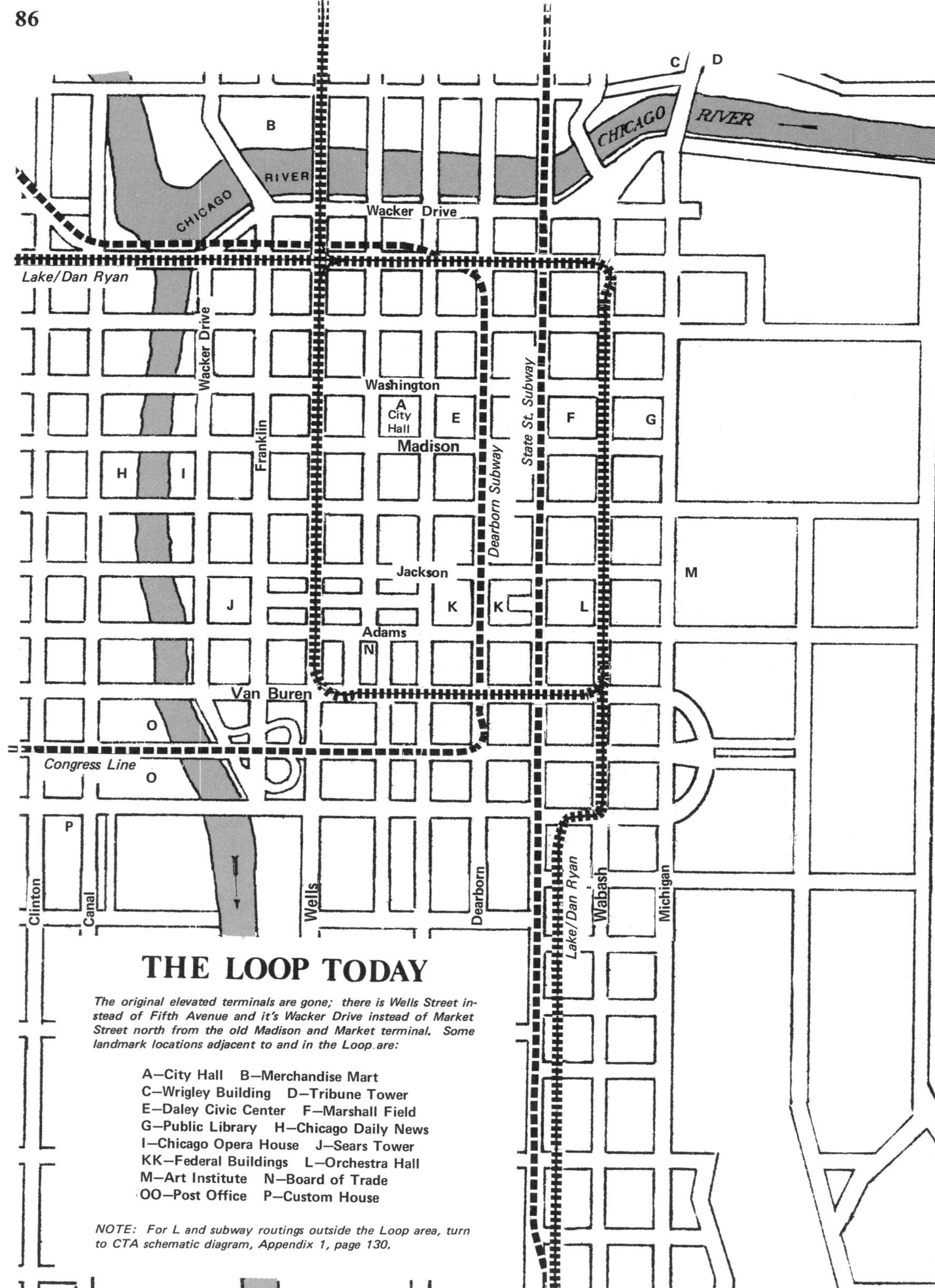

THE LOOP TODAY

The original elevated terminals are gone; there is Wells Street instead of Fifth Avenue and it's Wacker Drive instead of Market Street north from the old Madison and Market terminal. Some landmark locations adjacent to and in the Loop are:

A–City Hall B–Merchandise Mart
C–Wrigley Building D–Tribune Tower
E–Daley Civic Center F–Marshall Field
G–Public Library H–Chicago Daily News
I–Chicago Opera House J–Sears Tower
KK–Federal Buildings L–Orchestra Hall
M–Art Institute N–Board of Trade
OO–Post Office P–Custom House

NOTE: For L and subway routings outside the Loop area, turn to CTA schematic diagram, Appendix 1, page 130.

completed and Lake Street trains used the Wabash and Adams station as a stub terminal.

A second phase of construction, to get underway at some indeterminate time in the future, would entail an east-west subway under Monroe Street. This would give Lake Street trains underground access to downtown Chicago and finally permit complete demolition of the Loop. At some even more future date, this line could then tunnel northward at Michigan Avenue and head into the growing commercial and residential Lake Shore/Gold Coast area northeast of the Loop.

The overall effort to get started on something, anything, to replace the Loop acquired a sudden and shocking urgency brought about by one of the most extraordinary accidents in rapid transit annals. Shortly after 5:00 P.M. of a Friday, February 4, 1977, a train for Oak Park on the Lake-Dan Ryan line departed the Wabash and Randolph station, pulled through the tight Wabash-into-Lake curve and slammed head-on into the rear of a Ravenswood train at a standstill just beyond the turn. The four lead cars of the eight-unit train derailed, two of them crashing to the pavement below. Eleven passengers died, almost two hundred were injured. As CTA and City of Chicago crews labored to clear the line, one horribly tense moment was broadcast live on Chicago television. Cranes grappled with and lifted one car that had landed on its side in the street while all Chicago held its collective breath until the word came that no pedestrians had been caught beneath the 50,000-pound vehicle. L service was restored next day, and there was never any more intense discussion in Chicago about replacement subways than in the several days immediately following the calamity, even though it had been the only appallingly serious accident ever to befall the Union Loop throughout its existence up to that moment.[26]

Even as the C.U.T.D. staff commenced selecting engineers and contractors for the Franklin Street subway, a murmur of opposition began to be heard in Chicago, voices that questioned the wisdom of replacing the Union Loop. These doubters were in no sense against mass transit; rather they felt that the existing elevated structure, with modest investment in station amenities and some structural work here and there, can be useful for years to come. Then, there are the romantics who liken Chicago's downtown elevated line to what is left of the San Francisco cable-car network. Another group tries to equate the elevated structure as one with the Eiffel Tower. They say it would be a complete, final, total catastrophe to tear down so glorious an example from the years when man first began to use structural steel to remake the face of the earth. And there are even those who see in the plans to build a subway replacement for the Loop just one

Tragedy on the Union Loop. On February 4, 1977, an Oak Park-bound train on CTA's Lake-Dan Ryan line smashed into the rear of a Ravenswood train just beyond the Wabash-into-Lake curve, and this was the result. The Ravenswood train is the 6000 series cars to the right; the first four cars of the Lake-Dan Ryan train are off the structure, two of them lying on their side in the street. Eleven persons died in the mishap. (Copyrighted and used with the permission of the Chicago Tribune)

more instance of backroom political deals being made at the expense of daily transit riders.[27]

So much for theory. While it will surely not be the last word on the subject, any immediate threat to tear down the Loop has been quieted for the time being. In 1979 Chicago mayor Jane Byrne and Illinois governor James Thompson reached an agreement whereby the Franklin Street subway is to be cancelled, the elevated Loop retained and improved, and rapid transit improvements developed for residential sections of Chicago where such service is now substandard. Charles Tyson Yerkes' cleverly devised Union Loop has cheated the hangman once again. How long it will continue to do so is anybody's guess.

Builder's photo of CRT car No. 4251, a 76,800 pound motor car built by the Cincinnati Car Company in 1922. (Author's collection)

Right: End view of a CRT/CTA 4000 series car. Trolley enabled car to operate on suburban routes where overhead power collection was required. Alas, the conversion to conventional third rail of the last route so equipped doomed the 4000 series cars in 1974. See text, page 81.

Notes to Part Two

[1]Further information on the New York, Boston and Hudson & Manhattan subways can be found in the author's earlier books, all published by Stephen Greene Press of Brattleboro, Vermont: *Change at Park Street Under* (1972), *Under the Sidewalks of New York* (1979), and *Rails Under the Mighty Hudson* (1975).

[2]In 1915 George F. Swain, chairman of the Boston Transit Commission, suggested these cost ratios: Exclusive of equipment and land acquisition, a single track of surface line could be built for $50,000 per mile; elevated lines $250,000 per mile; subways at least one million dollars per mile. The *costs* date to Swain's estimates in 1915; the *ratios* are timeless. Swain, "Considerations with Regard to the Rapid Transit Problem in Cities," in *The Engineering Society of Western Pennsylvania*. (Volume XXXI, No. 3, April 1915), pp. 239–254.

[3]Chicago's network of cable railways, while smaller than San Francisco's in route miles, exceeded the city most identified with this novel form of transport in vehicles operated and in passengers carried per year. With this qualification, Chicago had the largest cable railway system in the nation and the world. For further details, see: George W. Hilton, *The Cable Car in America*. (Berkeley, California: Howell-North Books, 1971), pp. 234–249.

[4]Part Three, Chapter Fifteen.

[5]Arnold's first proposal recommended only a series of downtown subways for the city's streetcars. He argued, in 1902, that the capacity of the Union Loop could be increased inexpensively merely by lengthening the platforms at all downtown stations. His 1911 report to the City Council was the first to suggest replacing the Union Loop with downtown subways, as well as building an extensive tunnel network for streetcars. See Bion J. Arnold, *Recommendations and General Plans for a Comprehensive Passenger Subway System for the City of Chicago*. (Chicago: Chicago City Council, 1911).

[6]Old hands in Chicago still tell how absenteeism among the rank and file would be higher than usual on Election Day. In repayment for securing a position on the Ls or the street railways, one's "sponsor" would expect a day's work distributing circulars at the polls.

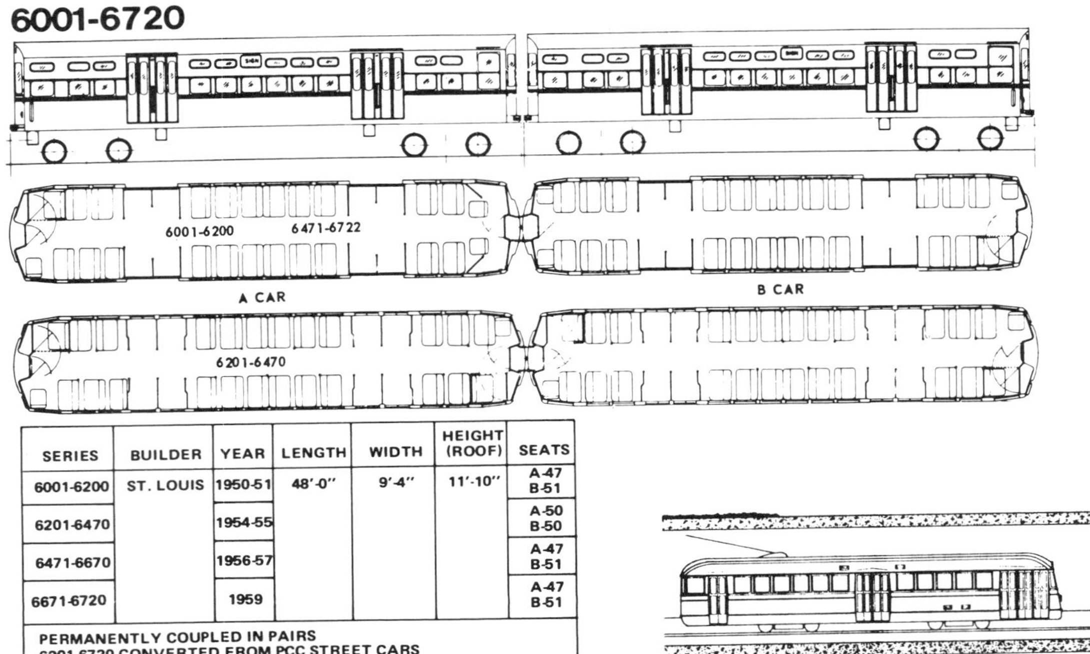

SERIES	BUILDER	YEAR	LENGTH	WIDTH	HEIGHT (ROOF)	SEATS
6001-6200	ST. LOUIS	1950-51	48'-0"	9'-4"	11'-10"	A-47 B-51
6201-6470		1954-55				A-50 B-50
6471-6670		1956-57				A-47 B-51
6671-6720		1959				A-47 B-51
PERMANENTLY COUPLED IN PAIRS 6201-6720 CONVERTED FROM PCC STREET CARS						

The statistics tabulated above are for the full 6000 series, although many of these cars have been retired in favor of later designs (see Appendices, pages 129 ff.). The inset drawing is a side view of Chicago's distinctive three-door PCC trolley car, shown as though operating in a subway. The PCC design influenced the 6000 series' look, and there was talk of a trolley subway as recently as 1937, but nothing ever came of it. (Author's collection)

[7]Interest in unification was not new. In 1908 the New York consulting firm of Ford, Bacon and Davis outlined a consolidated operating plan for M.B. Starring, then president of the Northwestern. The report also noted that the lines' stub-end terminals in downtown Chicago would be very useful in any unification, as the Union Loop was operating at or close to its absolute capacity.

Each of the four companies maintained a small terminal outside the Loop that was used, especially during rush hours, by excess trains that could not be accomodated on the Union Elevated. The South Side's original Congress Street terminal opened in 1892, the first day L trains operated in Chicago; the Lake Street line's original Madison and Market terminal opened in 1893; the Metropolitan had a terminal adjacent to Wells Street that opened in 1904 (after the line had begun running onto the Union Loop); and the Northwestern's stub-end depot on North Water Street, which opened in 1908, also after the company had initiated service around the Loop.

[8]Samuel Insull dictated his *Memoirs* in 1934 and 1935. They were never published, but his son, Samuel Insull, Jr., released limited copies of a notarized draft of his father's recollections in 1961.

[9]The Northwestern purchased the Union Elevated in 1904, thus reducing the original five companies to four.

[10]See Forest McDonald, *Insull.* (Chicago: University of Chicago Press, 1962), where this claim is advanced.

[11]James R. Quinn was one of the first people appointed to the Chicago Transit Board by Mayor Kelly in 1945, and he continued to serve faithfully in that post until his death on November 26, 1976, a month and a day shy of his eighty-sixth birthday.

[12]Approximately one hundred feet below the surface of downtown Chicago one reaches bedrock in a deposit called the Niagaran Dolomitic Limestone. This foundation has been in place for 300 million years, according to geologists, and its stability has allowed Chicago, in recent years, to construct some of the tallest buildings in the world. On top of this limestone are to be found layers of silty clay of a blue or gray color, and of differing consistencies. This clay was deposited during the last ice age, a "mere" 10,000 years ago. The uppermost layer throughout the Loop area consists of ten to fifteen feet of man-made fill that dates, essentially, to the 1871 fire.

First break from the design specifications used in the 6000 series cars came in 1964 when the CTA purchased two hundred cars from Pullman-Standard. Here is an artist's rendition of the new design, the first CTA rolling stock to be equipped with air-conditioners. (Author's collection)

[13]Longest "non-underground" railway platform in the world is the Kharagpu platform, West Bengal, India, 2,733 feet.

[14]For information on the Chicago Surface Lines, see: Alan R. Lind, *Chicago Surface Lines, an Illustrated History*. (Park Forest, Illinois: Transport History Press, 1974 and 1979). The 1979 edition contains a helpful chronology of the complex political maneuvering that led up to the public takeover of mass transit in Chicago. See pp. 444–473.

[15]Many important and civic-minded citizens have served on the Chicago Transit Board over the years, but only one of them ever hit 512 major-league home runs and is a member of the Baseball Hall of Fame. In 1969 Illinois governor Richard B. Ogilvie named Chicago Cubs shortstop Ernie Banks to fill an open position on the board. He served for over ten years.

[16]Planning for additional subways did not cease in Chicago when construction began on the State and Dearborn tunnels. In 1939 the City Council issued a tome-like report outlining an extensive system of new subway lines, including tearing down the eastern end of the Lake Street L and feeding it into the Dearborn subway.

[17]Although ordered while CRT was still in business, these units were designed by a committee of city, surface line and rapid transit staffers, in anticipation of the unification of all Chicago mass transit. Two were built by St. Louis Car Company, two by Pullman-Standard.

[18]Many PCC streetcars employ a similar braking system, but elsewhere in the world only the subway system in Hamburg, Germany, operates rapid transit cars with such an electrical-mechanical braking system. For additional information on the 6000 series cars, see: *Chicago's Rapid Transit*: Volume II, Rolling Stock, 1947–1976. (Chicago: Central Electric Railfans Association, 1976), especially pp. 8–61.

[19]The Congress Expressway was later renamed the Eisenhower Expressway. CTA, however, continues to call its transit line the Congress route.

[20]The North Shore negotiated this trackage rights arrangement with the CRT during the days when both companies were part of the Insull empure. See Part Three, Chapter Sixteen, for further details.

Mention subways in Chicago and one immediately thinks of the twin tubes built through the downtown area in the 1930s and 1940s. But there are others. To link the old Metropolitan L at Logan Square with the new median strip line in the Kennedy Expressway, a 1½-mile, two-station subway was built in 1970. This is the Belmont station. Another underground element of the CTA allows this same line access to O'Hare International Airport, an extension built in the early 1980s.

[21]The Congress Terminal was last used by the CTA in 1949, although North Shore interurbans used the facility for some time afterward. The Madison and Market terminal of the Lake Street L was phased out in 1909, returned to service in 1924, and finally abandoned in 1948. Elevated trains last boarded passengers at the Metropolitan's Wells Street terminal in August, 1948, although interurban trains of the Chicago, Aurora & Elgin used the facility until September 20, 1953. As noted in the text, L trains operated *through* this terminal, but did not stop at it, between 1955 and 1958. The North Water terminal of the Northwestern was last used on July 31, 1949.

[22]CTA likes to "balance" its through-routed rapid transit lines; thus, because the Dan Ryan portion generates heavier traffic than the Lake Street leg, CTA hopes to build a flyover at this point and pair the Dan Ryan with the Howard service via the State Street subway, then pair the Lake Street line with the South Side L via the Loop.

[23]Before its new cab signal system was installed in the mid-1970s, the Chicago Ls were surprisingly free of automatic signal protection. Subway tunnels were always so protected, of course, as were interlocking plants and a number of critical bottlenecks. On most of the elevated system, it was the judgment of motormen alone that kept trains safely spaced.

[24]Many engineers claim that because the long-term properties of structural steel were not so well known at the turn of the century, there was a tendency to "overdesign" structures like elevated lines. Overdesigned or otherwise, such structures have rewarded their designers with decades of dependable service.

[25]CTA's Skokie Swift still uses overhead power distribution, but not old fashioned trolley poles. See Part Three, Chapter Sixteen, for details.

[26]Likely the first mishap of any consequence on the Chicago Ls happened on the South Side on November 9, 1893, seventeen months after the line opened. A thick fog enveloped the city that morning, so that visibility was reported to be a mere twenty paces. At 22nd Street, adjacent to Friedburg's Opera House, steam locomotive No. 40 smashed into the rear of a stopped train. The locomotive tore half-way through the wooden car, but nobody was hurt.

[27]In a comment he intended to be off the record, a U.S. Department of Transportation official was embarassed to find himself quoted in the press with this assessment of the project to replace the Loop: "It's a real turkey."

PART THREE
Destination, Loop

CHAPTER FIFTEEN
The Freight Tunnels

NARROW-GAUGE RAILROAD BUFFS stalk the objects of their affection with uncommon zeal; they are a breed apart. Yet it's usually possible to stump the most dedicated aficionado with this poser: what was the two-foot gauge railway that owned 150 locomotives and more than 3,300 freight cars, operated over sixty-two miles of track, and was still in the common carrier business as late as 1959? Few railfans regularly swap photographs of this rare narrow-gauge railroad, for it was neither a steam-powered line that twisted its way through the Rocky Mountains nor one of the famous Maine two-footers. It was, rather, an electrified line that operated for over half a century under the streets of downtown Chicago. By all standards it was the Loop's most unusual rail operation. Thanks to its out-of-sight operating environment, few people ever saw it firsthand even if they knew about it.

The Chicago freight tunnels never enjoyed sound fiscal health; bankruptcies and reorganizations shadowed the operation all of its years. The original franchise granted in 1899 was not to build and operate a rail line at all, but to construct an underground conduit system for another novelty of the age—a telephone system. The basic tunnel configuration was a horseshoe-shaped bore seven and one half feet high and six and one half feet wide, designed to facilitate the hanging of metal brackets along the walls to support telephone cables. How and when the idea developed to convert the tunnels to freight hauling is uncertain. The construction got underway in 1901, but as late as 1903 an executive from the engineering section of the Illinois Telephone and Telegraph Company addressed the Western Society of Engineers, and he was still talking about cable conduits only. On the other hand, in April of 1902 reports appeared in the daily press hinting at a proposed new use for the abuilding tunnels.

The changeover from cable to freight tunnels was accompanied by a mind-boggling series of corporate realignments, watered stock issues, absentee ownership, and the filing of incorporation papers in such unlikely places as Trenton, New Jersey. Because of the invisible nature of the work—forty feet underground—few Chicagoans knew anything at all about these developments. Then, in the course of the year 1905, certain streets in the downtown area suddenly started sinking.

Preceding page: February, 1941, and much of the world is at war, but beneath the streets of downtown Chicago, workers toil building the city's long-awaited subway system. Here a new four-section articulated streamliner of the Chicago, North Shore & Milwaukee RR hammers across the diamond at Lake and Wells. Dubbed Electroliners, the North Shore's newest equipment likely marked the high-water mark for interurban design. Train is inbound from Milwaukee. (George Krambles Collection)

The technical reason for the sinking streets was simple enough to correct; most of the project's trunk-line tunnels were built under pressure (although without the use of boring shields) and these proved stable. But several cross-street connecting lines were mined without the benefit of an artificially pressurized airlock, and these were the locations where perceptible settling occured at street level. The city's Department of Public Works mandated the use of airlocks thenceforth on all construction. But the settling business also managed to bring the Chicago political establishment into the picture, and what had previously been a relatively quiet business deal became a public *cause célèbre*. City attorneys ruled the entire tunnel enterprise illegal at one point, and the City Council had to pass an ordinance correcting whatever shortcomings existed in the previous franchise instruments. Among the conditions spelled out in this action was a stipulation undoubtedly inspired by the elevated and surface-line operators: the underground freight tunnels must never carry passengers!

Following all this political maneuvering, another series of corporate realignments took place and, on August 15, 1906, the tunnels were formally opened as the right-of-way of a freight railroad. By 1910 the line had become something of an off-beat novelty in the engineering world, eliciting much comment in the trade press, of which the following is a fair example: "From an engineering standpoint it is to be regretted that a work of this magnitude should have been prosecuted without having the basis of a coherent and comprehensive plan."

Comprehensive plan or no, the tunnel railroad operated around a single major commodity—small package freight. Some 2,700 of the line's 3,300 cars were open-top, staked-sided good wagons designed to haul "less than carload lot" (l.c.l.) shipments.[1] This translated to a package delivery service in and out of downtown stores, but its most important function was to coordinate shipments bound for the score or more freight stations maintained near the Loop by conventional, standard-gauge railroad companies. The steam lines themselves were heavily into l.c.l. business at the time, and the freight tunnels proved to be an effective pipeline for such traffic to and from the many shippers in the Loop. And even from one railroad terminal to another.

For loading and unloading, the narrow-gauge cars were typically brought up from the forty-foot deep tunnels by elevators inside commercial buildings. In some cases, buildings had deep level sub-basements, and loading could take place there. A second kind of commodity routed over the system was coal, both the deliveries to downtown buildings and the removal of ashes. Another bulk shipment hauled from time to time was material excavated from new building sites in the Loop. Actually, during its own

Two glimpses of the "Illinois Underground Tunnel," as the freight tunnels are identified on one of these post card views showing a locomative and its crew ready for action at a complicated "Y" track formation.

At left: The Bion Arnold report (1911) took cognizance of the freight tunnels. In this cross section to scale the distance from railhead at street level to railhead in the freight tunnel measures 42'—6".

Below: A trainload of barrels rolls through one of the freight tunnels. Could be that one of the cars is loaded with beer kegs, as a bunghole in one of them, visible through the right hand arch, suggests. (Both photos from George Krambles Collection)

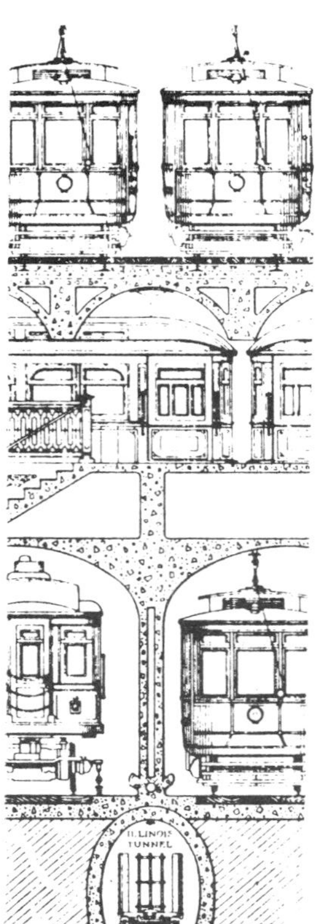

construction period, the tunnel system was used to funnel excavated material out of downtown over a temporary fourteen-inch-gauge railway system. Much of what is today Grant Park along Chicago's lake front was made with fill from the tunnels.

The tiny tunnels ran under virtually all major downtown streets, burrowed under the Chicago River and its south branch as often as necessary, and achieved a degree of fame in Chicago although seen and heard by few people. The weekly newspaper *Engineering News* speculated that had the freight delivery business been foreseen as the tunnels' principal function when they were planned, they might have been constructed to dimensions that would permit full size, standard-gauge freight cars to travel beneath Chicago's streets. On the other hand, the newspaper pointed out, "it seems doubtful whether a freight-handling system of the kind now developed would have been regarded as practicable at the time the tunnel system was first established, and a project for handling freight by an underground railway system would have received probably little support." In different language, a system like the Chicago freight tunnels could only have happened by accident!

Locomotives used in the freight tunnels operated on 250 volts of direct current drawn from an overhead trolley wire. A pilot installation in 1905 made use of a cog railway type of mine locomotive. This engine drew electricity from a third rail mounted between the running rails, but that was more than a mere power rail. It was a slotted device which did double duty as a rack for a gear-like wheel on the locomotive to engage to insure traction on grades. No such "insurance" proved necessary, however, so that conventional overhead trolley wire was soon substituted.

Operation in most of the tunnels was single-track in one direction only. This feature, plus a comprehensive book of rules, assured a safe and orderly operation.

The first major cutback of the system occurred when the City of Chicago set about its own subway building program in the late 1930s. The freight tunnels were relatively deep and it was thought they would remain safely below the grade of any passenger subway. In 1902, for instance, Bion Arnold ventured that the freight tunnels were of sufficient depth to allow a "single story" passenger subway to be built between the freight tunnels and the surface. However, Arnold felt that the freight tunnels would clearly preclude construction of any "two story" subways in Chicago. What happened, of course, is that while the Chicago passenger subways were built as "single story" affairs, they were also built at deep-bore level. City engineers had to dismantle the freight tunnels in the path of their boring shields under State, Dearborn and Lake streets. Crossing tunnels on perpendicular streets were also sealed off; and these were often backfilled with excavated materials from the new subway.

Ultimately it was the burgeoning of motor trucking that doomed the Chicago freight tunnels. Conventional railroads all but abandoned the l.c.l. business after World War II, and the over-the-road trucks that inherited this business were able to make door-to-door deliveries in the Loop, thus obviating the need for a specialized distribution system. Coal furnaces were converted to oil in large measure, and thus another specialty of the narrow-gauge line became obsolete. The end came quickly in 1959 amid all sorts of nostalgic plaints. Even today, an academic type will occasionally break into print with some suggestion to reopen the old freight tunnels. The bores apparently are inspected regularly since their structural integrity is important to engineers who must oversee the city's sewers, building foundations, and so forth. But the likelihood of their being returned to operation must be regarded as a long shot among long shots.

CHAPTER SIXTEEN

The Interurbans

IN THE HISTORY OF RAILWAY DEVELOPMENT worldwide, one singularly American contribution was the evolution of interurban lines in the early years of the twentieth century. Using the newly developed technology of electric traction, and often m.u. control as well, these lines became, in effect and sometimes in fact, intercity extensions of local trolley lines, providing an alternative, and often a more friendly and informal alternative, to the services provided by the steam railroads.

Furthermore, it can surely be claimed that no other transport industry has received the kind of careful and loving historical investigation as has the interurban. From volumes that treat the industry as a whole[2] to individual studies of virtually every interurban company from coast to coast, the bibliography is lengthy; each year it grows longer.

Three of the Midwest's more interesting interurban lines were also part of the sprawling Insull empire in the 1920s and merit inclusion in the story of the Chicago Loop. Each has been written about extensively on its own: the Chicago, Aurora & Elgin, nicknamed the "Roaring Elgin";[3] the Chicago, North Shore & Milwaukee[4] and the Chicago, South Shore & South Bend,[5] the latter two designated by the shorter and easier terminology, "North Shore" and "South Shore" respectively. Of this trio, two no longer operate.

Back in the days when it was not *the country's last interurban, a four car train zips across northern Indiana on the Chicago, South Shore & South Bend Railroad. Fourth car is a diner; observe the smoke drifting out, likely indicating some delicacy being prepared by the chef. (Author's collection)*

But by a strange and, some would say, marvelous turn of fate, the Chicago, South Shore & South Bend is still in business. Existing as a passenger carrier only by virtue of public subsidies, it appears to have beaten the odds and should survive into the foreseeable future. By most standards it is the country's last true interurban line. (Wars, schisms and divorces have resulted from lesser disputes about nomenclature, but it *should* be correct also to call the ex-Hudson & Manhattan line between New York and Newark, and which is currently operated by the Port Authority of New York and New Jersey, a true—and, likewise, a surviving—electric interurban. Traction buffs persist, however, in calling the South Shore the last of the breed.)

The South Shore gains entry into Chicago by means of a trackage rights arrangement that gives it access to the electrified suburban line of the Illinois Central Gulf Railroad.[6] That the Illinois Central Gulf Railroad *has*

The South Shore adopted a slogan from a popular children's story, and proudly displayed the legend on its cars and locos.

A two-car train of South Shore m.u. cars heads toward downtown Chicago over electrified trackage of the Illinois Central Gulf R.R. Three Insull-owned interurbans reached Chicago by virtue of trackage rights over somebody else's electrified railroad.

an electrified suburban line in and out of Chicago is itself more than an incidental matter and will be discussed in some detail in a later chapter. In any event, the South Shore uses the ICG for its Chicago access between 115th Street and the Loop, a distance of fourteen miles. While on ICG right-of-way South Shore trains are designated, by and for ICG towermen and dispatchers, with the numeral nine prefixed to their South Shore train number. Thus South Shore train No. 186 becomes No. 9186. At intermediate stations along the ICG line, the South Shore uses the same platform as the host railroad. For its downtown terminal, however, the South Shore has its own facility: a pocket-size depot, redolent of old-time interurban flavor, located adjacent to the ICG's own Randolph Street station. Both are east of Michigan Avenue, a short walk from the Adams-Wabash station of the Loop elevated.

The South Shore's efforts to hang on have been heroic.[7] The company even borrowed a theme from a famous bedtime story and decorated its cars and locomotives with the slogan: "the little railroad that could." The South Shore—now owned by the Chessie System, although it retains a good deal more of its traditional individuality than do other Chessie components—does a hefty freight business and has rail access to much of the heavy industry along the southern rim of Lake Michigan. It handles unit trains of coal, for instance, originated by other railroads and bound for power plants along the South Shore in the role of "terminating carrier." Although diesels now haul South Shore freight, the line was once famous for its variegated assortment of electric motors: veteran South Shore steeple-cab locomotives, ex-New York Central juice jacks, and Nos. 801, 802 and 803, the final surviving trio to haul tonnage electrically. These were the "Little Joes," so called, engines ordered from General Electric by the Soviet Union after World War II, but purchased by the South Shore when cold war tensions voided the sale. (The original Soviet order was for twenty units. GE sold five to Brazil, and the Milwaukee Road purchased twelve "Little Joes" for service in Montana, Idaho and Washington, an electrified district the railroad de-energized in 1974 and later abandoned outright.)

The "Little Joe" designation, incidently, is a reference to the premier of the Soviet Union, Yosif Vissarionvich Djugashvili, more commonly known as Joseph Stalin. It's more than slightly ironic that a man who may well have been the premier tyrant of the twentieth century has had his name memorialized on popular electric locomotives peacefully hauling freight on two American railroads.

At any rate, freight cushioned the impact of passenger losses over the years, and kept the South Shore alive until government assistance could inject some economic adrenalin.[8] The other two Insull interurbans lacked a

outh Shore's interurban heritage is evident in this view company's shops in Michigan City, Indiana. The ' has the shape and style of a typical trolley car barn. 'apanese-built m.u. cars will permit retirement of the -era equipment glimpsed in this scene.

To the uninitiated this may look like a diesel. But it isn't; it's South Shore electric locomotive No. 801, one of three "Little Joe" motors the road purchased from General Electric in 1949. Originally built for export to the Soviet Union, No. 801 served on the South Shore for over thirty years.

similar economic base. Consequently, these were abandoned before public subsidies for commuter rail services became available during the 1960s and '70s. Many observers in Chicagoland feel that both the Chicago, Aurora & Elgin and the North Shore would today be important elements of Chicago's subsidized commuter network had they, too, been rescued. They were not, and more's the pity.

All three interurbans had this in common: they operated into downtown Chicago by virtue of trackage rights over some other company's electrified right-of-way. For the South Shore, it used to be the Illinois Central Railroad, but now it's the Illinois Central Gulf, thanks to the merger of the IC with the Gulf, Mobile & Ohio. The other two lines secured entry over the lines of the Chicago Transit Authority and its predecessors. Thus the "Roaring Elgin" brought its trains in over the Garfield line of the Metropolitan West Side L and terminated just adjacent to the Loop at the Metropolitan's Wells Street terminal. Its operation did not actually extend onto the Union Loop itself, but that of the third interurban, the Chicago, North Shore & Milwaukee, did.

From a country interurban very much in the leisurely-service-along-the-side-of-the-road mold the North Shore was transformed into one of the country's speediest intercity rail links when it gained access in 1919 to downtown Chicago over the Northwestern L. Both the transit company and the interurban were, at the time, under Samuel Insull's control. Insull, who would again rely on Britton I. Budd as his operating officer, became chairman of the North Shore in 1916 when a protective committee of

OAK

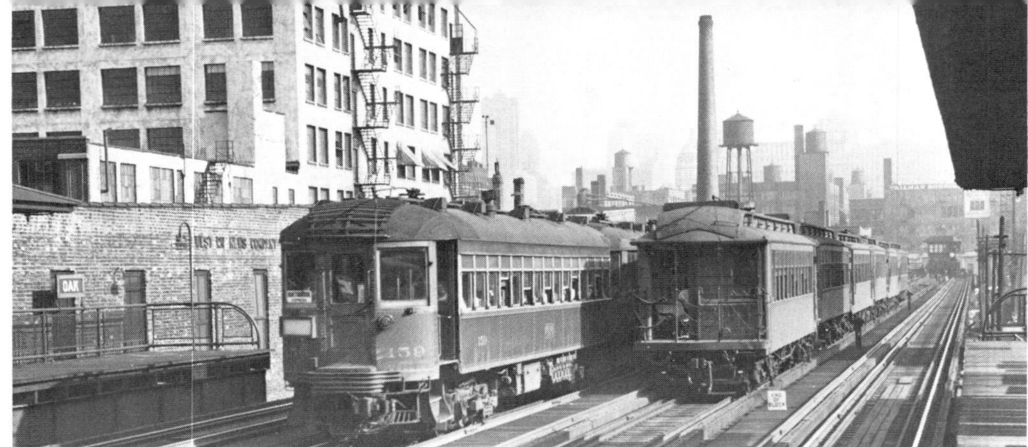

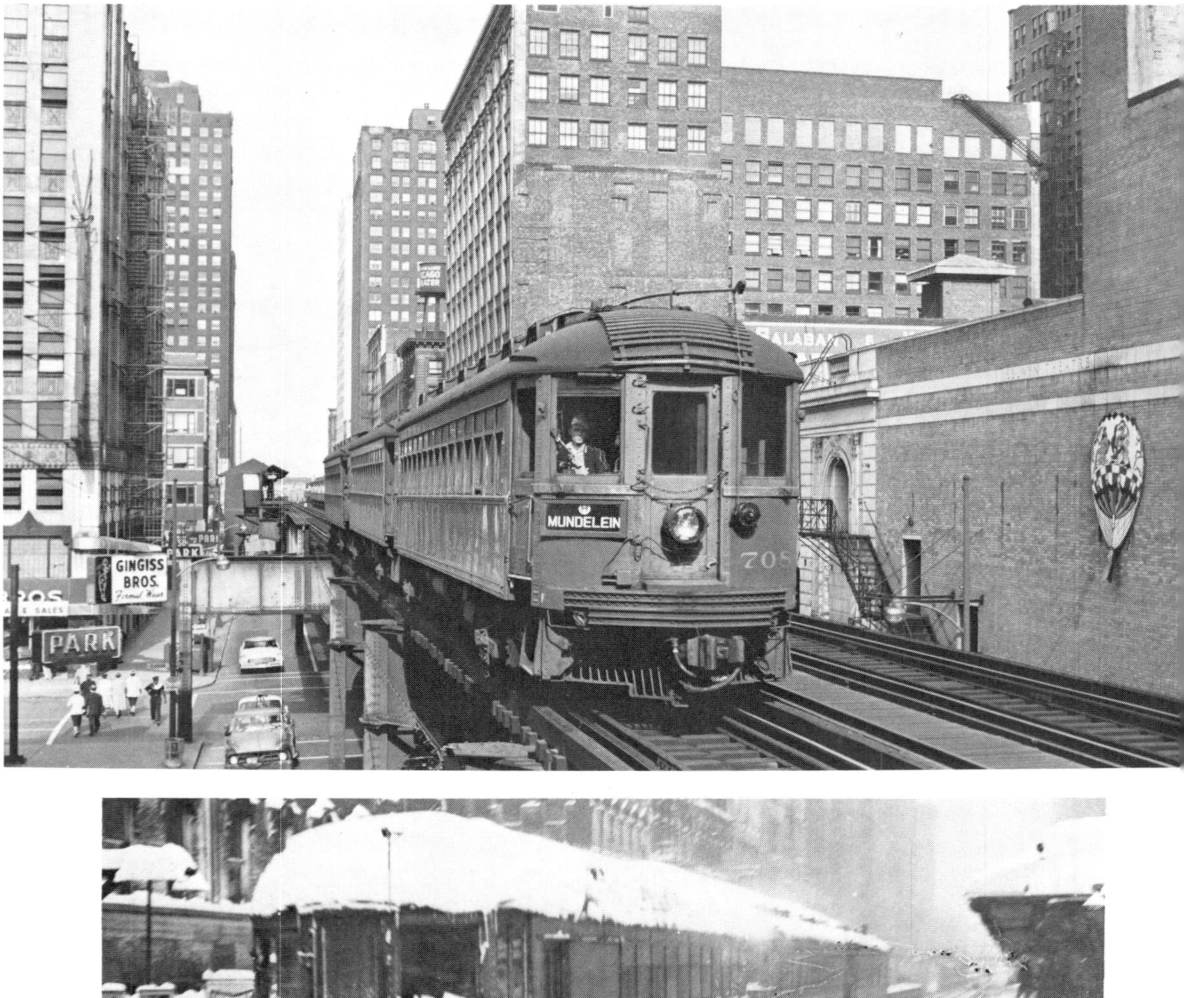
MUNDELEIN
GINGISS BROS.
PARK

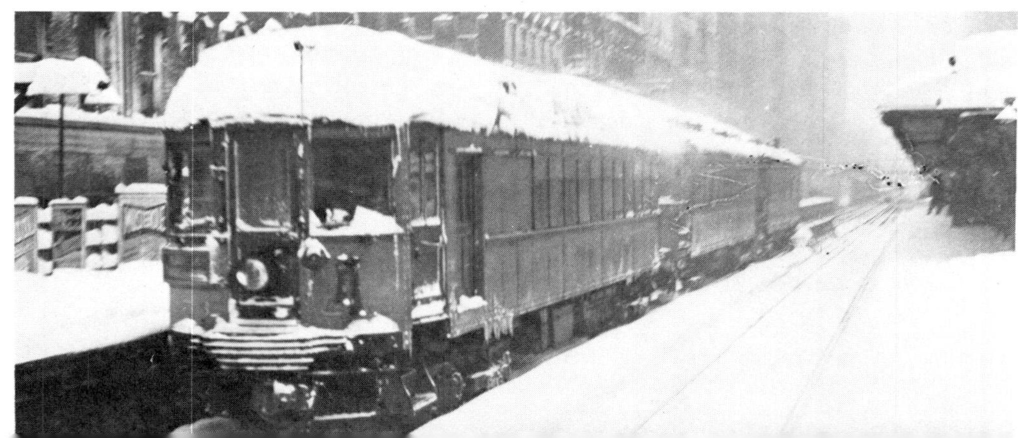

bondholders of the then bankrupt line asked him to step in and take charge. In other words, the railroad sought out Insull, a situation opposite to that which existed in the case of both the South Shore and the Chicago, Aurora & Elgin.

Insull himself looked upon these as likely investment opportunities. He wrote in his *Memoirs* that they "were acquired in the interest of the territory they served." Also, in the interest of Insull. For should the electric interurbans prove helpful in developing rural countryside into populous settled suburbs, all would prove beneficial to Insull's electric power enterprises. A further tie-in between power companies and railways was that the latter afforded the former ready-made rights-of-way for transmission lines. Interestingly, although Insull eventually was the "top dog" on both the CRT and the Chicago, Aurora & Elgin, the interurban had

osite page: SCENES FROM THE HEYDAY OF THE NORTH SHORE

: When North Shore interurbans headed out of Chicago over the Northwestern L bound "company iron" at the Chicago city line, the fine four-track structure that Charles Tyson kes built allowed the interurbans to make good time, yet not interfere with CRT/CTA ice. On June 29, 1949, a North Shore train bound for Northbrook, Illinois, passes a p-bound L train at Oak Street. (George Krambles Collection)

ay, the Union Loop serves only rapid transit trains of the Chicago Transit Authority. But that many years ago, the facility also saw periodic service by interurban trains of the cago, North Shore & Milwaukee Railroad. Here in 1958, a three car North Shore edule heads west along the Lake Street leg of the Union Loop, bound for Mundelein, ois. (George Krambles Collection)

tom: January 1939, and a fiece winter storm is belting the Middle West. But interurban ns continue to run on the Chicago, North Shore & Milwaukee Railroad. Here a hbound three-car schedule moves north along the Wabash Avenue leg of the Union p. Milwaukee is ninety-odd miles ahead, and one can guess that the trip may well have un a little late on this day. (George Krambles Collection)

negotiated its entry into Chicago over the Garfield L long before Insull came on the scene. The first interurban train of what was then called the Aurora, Elgin & Chicago Railway, which itself was part of an electric railway complex that included local and intercity trolley lines in the Fox River Valley west of Chicago, reached the Wells Street Terminal in 1905. The Insull takeover severed the corporate link with local streetcars in Elgin and Aurora and, with that move, the Chicago, Aurora & Elgin Railroad became the interurban's proper name.[9]

Under Insull management the North Shore first reached downtown Chicago over the CRT in 1919. For most of its existence, the company's trains circuited the Loop in the manner of regular L trains through-routed from the Northwestern to the South Side. That is to say, southbound service from Milwaukee to Chicago entered the Loop at Tower 18, continued south over the Wells Street leg, then turned east on Van Buren. Trains then swung south again at Wabash onto the old Alley L, and wound up at a station which was located where the South Side crossed Roosevelt Road. Interurban cars laid over between runs on portions of the three-track elevated line south of this point. As was noted earlier, between 1949 and the North Shore's eventual abandonment in 1963, the interurban line was the sole user of the elevated entry onto the Loop that was originally part of the South Side L, all other rapid transit trains from the South Side having been routed into the State Street subway. The North Shore also used the stub-ended Congress terminal as a freight and baggage depot after CTA phased out its regular L operations in 1949.

One significant exception to this general arrangement prevailed between 1922 and 1938. During this interval, the Chicago, North Shore & Milwaukee did more than merely reach the Loop area of downtown Chicago; trains continued over the South Side elevated system all the way to Jackson Park.

The "Roaring Elgin" and the North Shore had many similarities, similarities dictated by technical constraints imposed by clearances and other features of the Chicago Ls. Each company developed equipment with side walls bulging outward above platform level, thus providing rolling stock of maximum capacity. (The CTA would later use the same technique in designing its 6000 series fleet.) Also, though equipped for drawing direct current from trackside third rail on CRT/CTA right-of-way, both interurbans were able to switch to overhead trolley wire elsewhere. The North Shore used trolley pickup over virtually all its own trackage, while the CA&E employed third rail on private right-of-way and used overhead wire only while running on city streets in places like Aurora and Elgin.

The South Shore line, by contrast, uses an electrical system compatible with Illinois Central's electrification. Pantographs, instead of trolley poles, draw 1,500 volts of direct current from an overhead catenary system. Not having to transit the elevated Loop, and boasting a right-of-way engineered to main line railroad standards, South Shore rolling stock has not had to conform to rapid transit's limiting dimensions. A typical Chicago, Aurora & Elgin car was forty-seven feet long and eight feet, six inches wide. South Shore stock is ten feet wide, and while some cars are sixty-one feet long, others measure more than seventy-five feet from end to end.

Both the North Shore and the "Roaring Elgin" served important suburban communities outside Chicago. But the CA&E's longest line extended only to Aurora, thirty-eight miles from State and Madison, whereas the CNS&M operated all the way to Milwaukee, almost ninety miles away. North Shore trains managed the trip in as little as ninety-five minutes. A major capital improvement carried out during the Insull regime provided the railroad with a right-of-way that as much as any other single improvement made such high-speed performance possible. This was the opening of the Skokie Valley route in 1925. The interurban's original line north out of Chicago hugged the densely populated Lake Michigan shore and was hampered by frequent grade crossings and other impediments to swift service. The Skokie Valley line was a supplementary inland route for through service that was built to facilitate fast running. In all the pages of his *Memoirs* devoted to electric railroading, Insull gives more space to the construction of this by-pass route between Chicago and Lake Bluff than to any other accomplishment.

FROM "SKOKIE VALLEY" TO "SKOKIE SWIFT"

The demise of the two interurbans was a bitter ending for both. Each went its separate corporate way after the Insull debacle in 1932, and succeeded in posting impressive ridership statistics during the gasoline rationed years of World War II. After that, decline. In 1958 the North Shore first petitioned to abandon outright. Court battles, regulatory hearings, an aborted effort to turn the line into a passenger-owned cooperative—

In early 1982 something happened on the South Shore that last took place when Herbert Hoover was in the White House: a new interurban car was delivered to the road! Car No. 1—shown here during a trial run at the Nippon Sharyo plant in Toyokawa, Japan—is the first of a 36-car order placed by the Northern Indiana Commuter Transportation District. Car No. 1 reached the U.S. via the port of Philadelphia and arrived at the South Shore's Michigan City, Indiana, shops on January 26, 1982. (American Public Transit Association)

all these served merely to stay the date of execution. The end came in January, 1963. David Morgan, editor of *Trains* magazine, remarked that no action in his memory so infuriated the railfan community as the shutdown of this famous interurban. Its final day was one so bitterly frigid that several cases of frostbite were reported by railfans out to capture the line's final hours on film. Many such efforts were sadly unsuccessful, as camera shutters also froze in temperatures hovering close to zero.

Even before the North Shore abandonment, the planning office of the Chicago Transit Authority began to ponder some ideas as to how that portion of the line that served suburban communities north of Chicago might be incorporated into the CTA system. As time went on, and no agency was found willing to underwrite the costs, the Authority's plans never reached fruition.

The closing of the Chicago, Aurora & Elgin had some ironic and dramatic aspects. A plan to upgrade and improve Chicago mass transit became the proximate cause of the line's demise. As described earlier, the interurban line made its entry into Chicago over the tracks of the Metropolitan's Garfield L. (The two companies also worked out a cooperative plan to extend rapid transit service out beyond the end of the CRT right-of-way to provide local service to communities that were technically on the interurban route.) Following World War II, plans began to firm up to build a major new highway west out of downtown Chicago, the Congress Expressway, with a transit right-of-way in the median strip. That this new line would replace the Garfield L was not a problem. What did cause concern, however, was the necessity of tearing down large sections of the older L before the median strip right-of-way would be available. During the many months of construction, CTA L trains could temporarily survive on a grade-crossing plagued street-level right-of-way, but the CA&E people felt otherwise, that in fact such an expedient would, for them, be impossible.

The resulting compromise was flawed from the start. The CA&E cut back service from the Loop to Forest Park, establishing a temporary terminal at the end of the Garfield L in 1953. The company's Chicago-bound passengers were thus required to transfer to the CTA for a ride over the temporary street-level route to the Loop. The interurban trains themselves were kept free of the street-level route, but their passengers were forced not only to endure the delays, but to suffer the nuisance of changing trains in order to do so. The "Roaring Elgin" lost considerable business to competing commuter railroads, which were then investing in new air-conditioned rolling stock. The line abandoned all passenger service in 1957. Its freight service, never very robust, was eliminated in 1961, and thus another interurban faded from the scene.

Title to the company's assets passed to a salvage firm, Commercial Metals, of Dallas, Texas. A diesel locomotive, chartered from U.S. Steel's Chicago "Outer Belt" railroad, the Elgin, Joliet & Eastern, powered the work train that dismantled the line. The salvage firm also tried to back out of several deals railway museums had negotiated to purchase several of the road's old interurban rolling stock. But the museums would not be denied. They banded together, hired an attorney, and as a result posterity will long be able to appreciate the style of equipment that once ran on this famous line.[10]

The North Shore, incidently, saw two of its more famous trains return to active service on another electric railway. In 1941 the company took delivery from St. Louis Car Company of two four-section articulated units dubbed the "Electroliners"—which may well have represented the high-point of interurban design in this country. They were purchased in 1963 by the Red Arrow Lines, a company now part of the Philadelphia area's publicly-operated mass transit agency. The units ran for several seasons over that company's third-rail line between Norristown, Pennsylvania, and the 69th Street Terminal of the Market Street subway-elevated. Renamed "Libertyliners" for service in Philadelphia, the twin articulated trains spent considerable time out of service and were never able to recapture the glory they saw on the North Shore. Philadelphia may have a greater variety of electric railways than any other place in America. Local pride, however, surely could not have been well served when rail buffs would travel considerable distances to see and ride, not the indigenous equipment, but a pair of outlanders from the Middle West.

As it would later do with the North Shore, CTA developed an operating plan for incorporating all or some of the CA&E into the rapid transit system. A unique proposal was included for equipment: CTA suggested converting some of its pre-war PCC streetcars for that purpose. These were not the *post*-war cars that became instrumental in building the 6000 series rapid transit cars, but older vehicles. They would have made quite an impression rolling west into suburban communities of Cook and Dupage counties, but failure to develop a funding source doomed the plan. The pre-war PCCs were dispatched to the scrap heap.

One little "chapter" should be added to the story of the Insull interurbans, although it is far from a "little" accomplishment. The CTA was indeed unsuccessful in establishing rapid transit service over any large portion of either the North Shore or the CA&E. But in 1964, thanks to funds made available through a demonstration grant from Washington, the CTA reinstituted service over a 4.9-mile segment of the old North Shore line as a feeder link to its own rapid transit system, and named it the

"Skokie Swift." It operates into the suburban village of Skokie, which is just beyond the Chicago city limits in north suburban Cook County, and was once part of Insull's high-speed Skokie Valley line. The "demonstration" proved worthwhile beyond CTA's wildest hopes so that "the Swift" has since been made a permanent part of the CTA system. Although it is physically connected to the basic CTA network, it is exclusively a feeder shuttle route, running single-car trains back-and-forth between Dempster and Howard stations. Now, under the provisions of the labor agreement between CTA and the Amalgamated Transit Union, single-car trains require but a single on-board crew member, who serves as both motorman and conductor. Here's where productivity and nostalgia make common cause; because a multi-section articulated *unit* falls under the contract definition of a single *car*, the experimental trains that were ordered back in the final days of the CRT survive in rush-hour service on the Skokie Swift. They are subjected to an extraordinary amount of tender loving care by CTA shop forces and, as with other cars assigned to this service, have been equipped with a unique bow-style overhead power collector enabling trains to switch from third rail to trolley wire catenary automatically and on the fly.

The Skokie Swift, at 4.9 miles, is hardly more than a shadow of the North Shore's ninety mile right-of-way to Milwaukee. But it's better than nothing at all, and talk is continually heard of extending the line beyond its current terminal at Dempster Street to a major regional shopping center a mile or so further north.[11]

CHAPTER SEVENTEEN
Two If By Sea

HARKENING BACK to our Introduction's word-association exercise, it is hardly to be expected that "Chicago" would trigger the response word, "seaport." Technically, courtesy of the St. Lawrence Seaway, Chicago is entitled to the appellation. Even if one remembers that Chicago is a lake port accommodating many ships each year, it is cargo rather than people that these vessels transport, and there is no glamorous connotation as evoked by New York or Boston, each with its established maritime traditions and the coming and going of "ocean greyhounds" or luxury cruise ships.

Back around the turn of the century the Goodrich Transit Company and similar firms operated passenger vessels out of Chicago to cities elsewhere on Lake Michigan, but the majority of these passengers-only craft berthed along the Chicago River—a waterfront easily accessible on foot from both Loop and subway stations on Lake Street—have been excursion craft designed for a day's out-and-back recreational cruising, not vessels engaged in basic point-to-point transportation.

Parenthetically, one such sailing in June 1915 culminated in one of the world's major maritime disasters and the most grievous transportation mishap of any sort in or near the Loop. The passenger steamer *Eastland*, 1,961 tons, 256 feet long, built in 1903, was being eased away by a tugboat from her slip at La Salle Street and the Chicago River. Aboard were 2,400 employees of the Western Electric Company, and their families, intent on a carefree picnic outing. Intrigued by the intricate departure maneuver, the passengers crowded onto the upper decks and to the side of the boat where they could see what was happening, whereat the *Eastland* capsized! The death toll numbered 835, more than a third of those aboard. Coming as it did only five weeks and three days after the *Lusitania* was torpedoed off the Irish coast, the disaster gave the nation in general, and Chicago in particular, a jittery awareness of perils afloat.

Despite lack of tradition in passenger transportation by water, there is, wonder of wonders, an active common-carrier maritime service exclusively for passengers, operating over a regular route, so that Chicago is today one of the rare places in America whose basic urban transporation system includes a waterborne element. Right on the edge of the Loop itself!

Each year from April through October the Wendella Company, whose principal business is the operation of sightseeing cruises out into Lake Michigan, provides a rush-hour service on the Chicago River between the Chicago & North Western depot and North Michigan Avenue. The service began in 1963, although not without objection from CTA. The authority claimed its enabling legislation gave it the exclusive right to operate scheduled passenger service on "public ways" in Chicago. The ensuing debate turned on whether the brackish waters of the Chicago River constituted such a thoroughfare. Free enterprise won out. Established with a little introductory assist from the Chicago & North Western Railway, the service continues with several trips in both the morning and evening rush hours. The vessels are neither workaday ferryboats nor magnificent palace steamers bedecked with gilded gingerbread trim, but are smallish single-deck motor boats. Thanks to traffic congestion that frequently delays CTA buses plying to and from the North Western depot, the Wendella sight-seeing yachts are often the fastest way for commuters to reach their trains. But more importantly, passengers can enjoy the leisurely respite of an airy ten-minute cruise beyond comparison with even the most comfortable air-conditioned bus in the CTA fleet. The Wendella "fleet" comprises two craft, the *Sunliner* and the *Wendella.* Reader, pause and reflect; they are the only units in Chicago's mass transit network that operate without benefit of public subsidy.

CHAPTER EIGHTEEN

Railroads To The Loop

ALTHOUGH THE WENDELLA VESSELS REMAIN to be the last portion of the Loop's urban transport system to be operated fully by the private sector in the classic free enterprise pattern, when the two boats began service in 1963 they enjoyed no such exclusivity. Indeed, even the CTA, while publicly owned and operated, was mandated by law to meet all ordinary operating expenses out of farebox revenue. This the agency managed to do from its inception after World War II until about 1970. The difference, of course, between a CTA paying its expense out of income and a CRT in hopeless receivership was that the public agency didn't have to pay either taxes or amortization charges on equipment and its other assets. Capital investment—i.e., new buses and L cars—was handled by separate accounts and did not have to be paid out of the farebox. But routine day-to-day expenses did; as a result Chicago's basic transit fare was generally much higher than similar tariffs in Boston and New York during the 1950s and 1960s. Then, with the dawn of the 1970s the fabric started to unravel; the farebox could no longer keep pace with ever rising costs. Direct operating subsidies from the public treasury became necessary.

The same economic factors that forced a realignment of public support and subsidy for CTA in the mid-1970s also spelled major changes for another key element of the region's passenger transport system: suburban commuter service betweeen the Loop and outlying communities by privately operated, profit-seeking railroads. The decade of the 1970s saw not only the shift of railroad commuter service from private to public, there was also the coming of Amtrak, a national public agency created to preserve intercity rail passenger service from extinction in the United States. How these developments impinged on rail mass transportation in and around downtown Chicago is germane to the story of the Loop.

To capsulize the railroads of Chicago in a short chapter is impossible. Actually, just the railroad *depots* of Chicago would make a subject deserving of a book by itself, as, for instance one similar to the volume Alan Jackson has produced about the several railway terminals in London.[12] One or two of the railroads involved in commuter operations out of Chicago have been the subject of individual studies of their overall operations. In all of these treatments, however, commuter services have represented relatively so small a part of total corporate activity that they have received scant attention.[13]

Many of Chicago's railroads were, and remain, prosperous companies. Consequently several Chicago roads were able to afford postwar capital investment in their commuter operations, something which did not happen to any measurable degree elsewhere in the country, particularly in the east. Not only was older equipment replaced with new, but a totally different kind of technology was developed for the commuter lines.

As a general rule in the United States, the process of change from steam to diesel locomotives after World War II was not carried to its logical conclusion in regard to passenger trains. Because of a need to retain full compatibility between, one, the older steam locomotives, two, the newer diesels, and three, the cars they hauled, steam continued to be used for car heating. Steam heating was a natural by-product when steam engines hauled the nation's trains, but it had to be specially provided for when diesels replaced the older form of power. Thus the new diesels had to be equipped with auxiliary steam boilers, and even brand-new passenger cars continued to be fitted out with complex car-to-car piping for delivery of this steam, plus car-borne batteries and axle-connected generators for powering lights and other electrical functions. But a diesel locomotive is, in fact, a diesel-electric, in which the diesel engine drives an electric generator, which in turn supplies direct current for traction motors that drive the wheels—with enough left over to provide current for auxiliary services aboard passenger cars. Two heavy, messy, and maintenance-prone systems—steam and batteries—could thus have been eliminated. But they weren't, so that, in general practice on U.S. passenger trains, steam heating continued as the norm well on into the diesel era.

After World War II, when several of the Chicago railroads took up the matter of replacing their worn out and outdated commuter fleets, they realized that any need for full compatibility with long-haul intercity equipment was a thing of the past. For once they could design a car from scratch and seek to achieve not only the ideal for high-density suburban service, but also take advantage of the inherent assets of the new diesel-electric locomotives.

We must credit the manner in which Chicago Union Station assesses

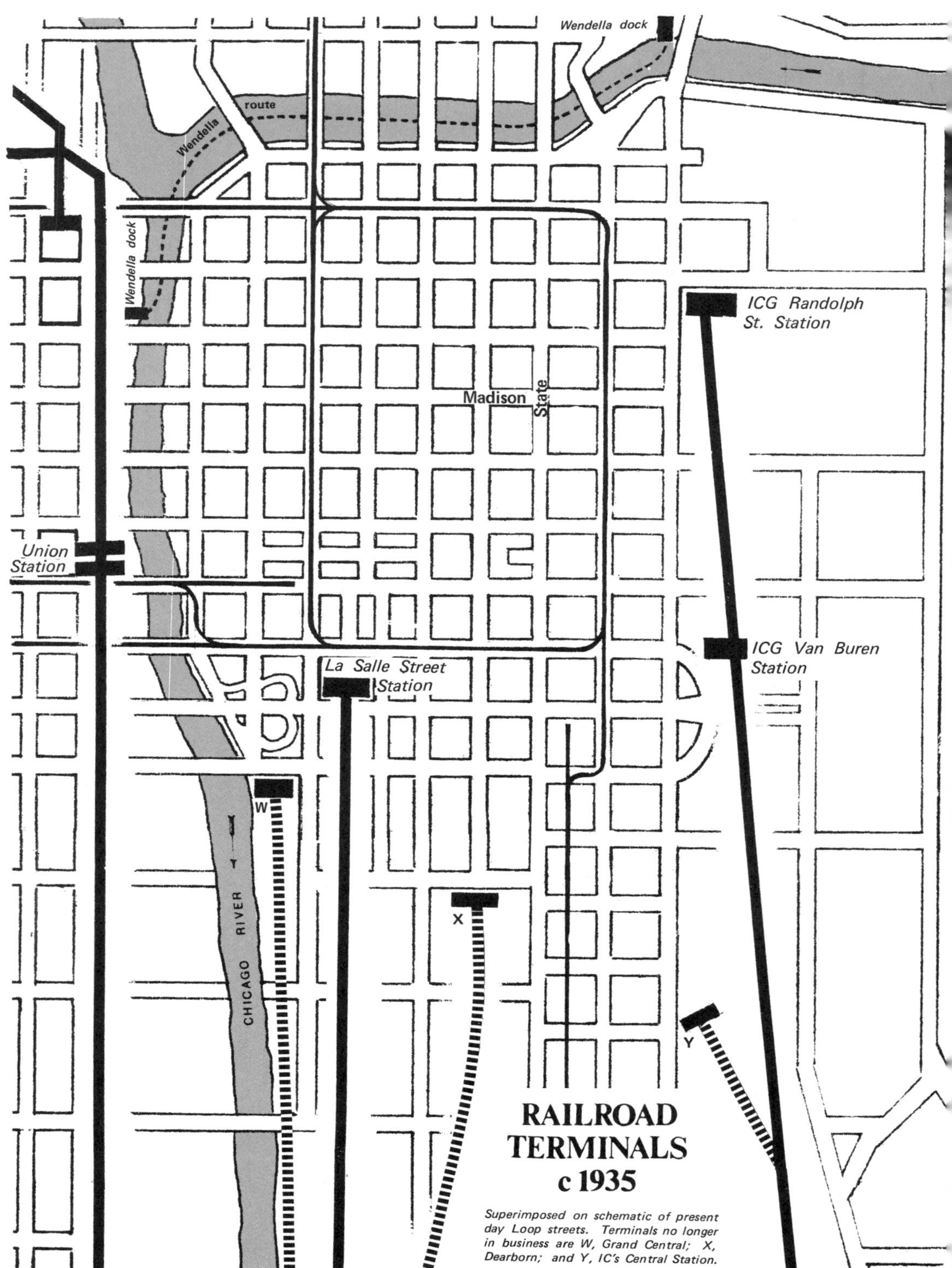

RAILROAD TERMINALS c 1935

Superimposed on schematic of present day Loop streets. Terminals no longer in business are W, Grand Central; X, Dearborn; and Y, IC's Central Station.

"user charges" to its participating railroads for a share in this evolution. Each train movement in and out of CUS, in revenue service, subjects the railroad involved to a "wheelage charge": the more wheels, the higher the toll. Thus, for Chicago, the ideal commuter car should be one that can seat more passengers "per wheel," enough to attain a decided economic edge over conventional rolling stock. Then why not a two-level car? . . .

Unfortunately, in and around Chicago, clearances rule out the use of a genuine two-level vehicle. Behold, then, the gallery car! In a typical example of the design the floor level provides conventional 2–2 seating on either side of a center aisle. The "upper deck" is a gallery, not a separate level. Actually, there are four galleries per car. They extend out over the floor seats, balcony style, but not over the aisle. Each gallery itself has a small aisle flanked by single seats. Passengers on the main level must stoop a little, but not a lot, to get in and out of their seats. But in the main aisle—why, Wilt Chamberlain and Ralph Sampson can stand erect and still have plenty of headroom! The car ceiling itself is close to twelve feet high.

Passengers board gallery cars through a mid-car vestibule. One of the few differences between the gallery cars of various railroads involves whether the entry and exit doors accommodate two "streams" of passengers (e.g., Burlington) or three (e.g., every other railroad). Just inside the passenger compartments spiral staircases provide access to the galleries. These stairways are not outstandingly difficult to navigate; nevertheless, Dashiell Hammett's Thin Man would find getting up to the gallery a good deal easier than Rex Stout's Nero Wolfe. A typical gallery car provides seats for some 160 passengers, two-thirds of them in the car's floor seating, the rest upstairs.

All Chicago gallery cars are air-conditioned, with the apparatus located over the center vestibule; electrical power comes from the locomotive. Thus, without the cumbersome batteries and generators that had long been the characteristic features of American railroad passenger cars, car weight has been kept to tolerable limits despite a distinctly big and bulky look. The average gallery coach weighs about 100,000 pounds, versus 90,000 or so for a one-deck "steam and battery" coach of equivalent length.

One little glitch developed when engineers began to get serious about using electricity from diesel locomotive to power train lighting; on early model diesel locomotives they found it not feasible to tap directly into the main generator. So the roads mounted an auxiliary diesel and generator in the back of the locomotives where the steam boilers used to be. These produced what is now called "head-end power." (The inevitable abbreviation: HEP.) Later, when new locomotives were ordered for Chicago commuter service, it had become possible for the manufacturer to combine the separate functions of both the main and auxiliary diesels into the prime mover.

A fleet of gallery cars includes two kinds of units: ordinary trailer cars and control cab cars. The latter take advantage of yet another feature of the diesel locomotive, its ability to be operated "from a distance," i.e., the opposite end of the train. A train includes a locomotive on one end and a control cab car on the other, so that an engineer can operate his train from either end without shifting the locomotive. "Push-pull" is the ordinary designation for this style of operation, and it has brought about an enormous reduction in the unproductive switching needed to get a locomotive from one end of a train to the other.

Thus in the twilight of private investment in railway passenger service there evolved a near-perfect innovation for meeting one city's particular needs in commuter service between downtown and the suburbs. While the preceding description applies generally to Chicago's several suburban fleets, the technology's application on specific railroads has brought several interesting variations on the norm.

The Chicago, Burlington & Quincy Railroad—a corporation that has since been merged into the present-day Burlington Northern—has long operated commuter service over its main line between Chicago Union Station and Aurora, Illinois, thirty-eight miles away. The Burlington actually *invented* the gallery car when, in 1948, it ordered the first of the species from the Budd company. CB&Q specified an HEP electrical system for its original fleet, but stayed with conventional steam for car heating. The reason? The railroad powered its suburban trains with locomotives from its intercity pool, engines which had to be able to provide steam-for-heating anyway, so the older style system was retained. Each train of gallery cars had to include one specially rigged conventional coach that contained a small diesel engine for powering train lighting. This initial investment was made with corporate funds only, no public subsidies.

The region's largest, and the country's second largest, commuter service is operated by the Chicago & North Western Railway. The company began to dabble in gallery technology in 1955 when it purchased sixteen cars from the St. Louis Car Company. They were not, at first, rigged for push-pull service. Later, when C&NW decided to re-equip its entire suburban fleet, it inaugurated a massive program requiring 264 additional cars, of which sixty-four were control cab cars for push-pull runs. These were bought from Pullman-Standard, and the original sixteen from St. Louis were rebuilt to train with the rest of the new fleet. Unlike Burlington's stainless steel units,

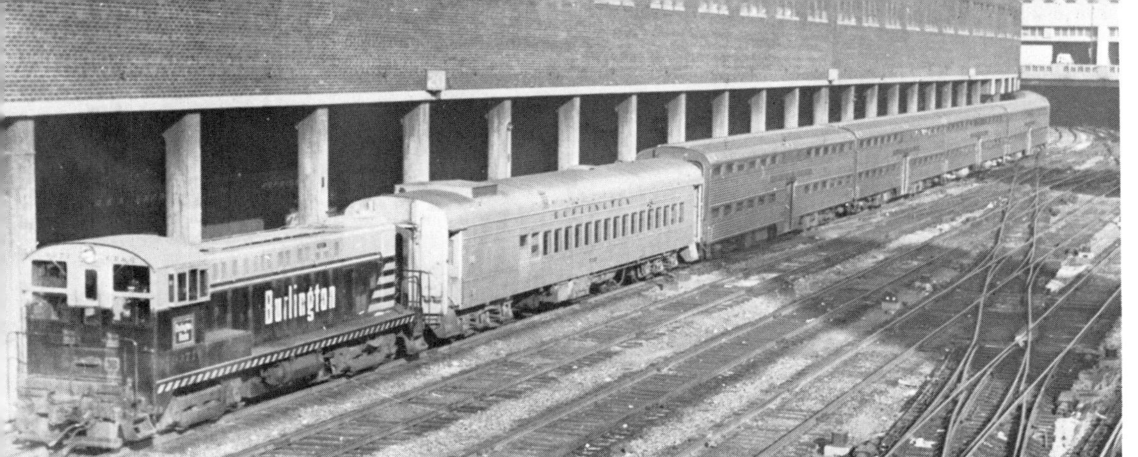

r almost twenty years, the Burlington Northern—and before it, the Chicago, Burlington & Quincy RR—erated its suburban service without benefit of public subsidy. Its gallery cars required head-end electric power t, because the railroad hauled commuter trains with locomotives from its intercity pool, it had to rig some ıgle-deck coaches with auxiliary generators to provide this power. Note the roof hatch on the oddball car in the ıin hauling out of Union Station behind a switcher in this 1965 view. That's where the diesel generator's cated.

C&NW gallery cars are of conventional steel construction, which the railroad has painted in company colors, green and bright yellow.

Chicago & North Western's investment in commuter services paid an unusual dividend: after pruning a few unproductive elements, the suburban operation was able to remain "in the black" until 1974, setting a record for profitability. Certainly it is the last U.S. urban rail service of any scale entitled to make such a claim.[14] The railroad operates three lines out of Chicago: one due north, one to the northwest, and one to the west, all of them three-tracked in their heavily trafficked zones. The line to the northwest has a backwoodish single-track branch that leaves the main line near Crystal Lake, Illinois, and meanders north. Until recently it served the fashionable resort of Lake Geneva, Wisconsin, but has lately been cut back to the Illinois side of the Wisconsin state line. Also unique to the C&NW is the fact it operates "left-handed," British style, in multiple-track territory

The Roosevelt Road viaduct in Chicago has long been, and remains, a fine place to watch trains coming and going. Outbound from Union Station behind a rebuilt E9 type diesel, a five-car train of gallery cars heads for Aurora, Illinois, over the Burlington-Northern RR, in 1975.

(as did Charles Tyson Yerkes' two elevated lines). Many new residents in C&NW land get a shock when they arrive at the depot for their first morning's commute into Chicago. "Why are all those people waiting on the outbound platform?" the newcomer asks. The answer comes when the 8:12 train drifts into town on the "wrong" track.

Left-handed or not, Chicago & North Western operates its commuter fleet in what has become the Chicago standard: locomotive on the "outbound" end of the train and a control cab car on the "city" end. Thus enginemen—and soon, "enginepersons"—ride the diesel when heading towards the suburbs, but operate from the quiet of the control cab when trains are Chicago bound.

Engine crews have mixed views of their job when it comes to working aboard a locomotive or working in a control cab car. The latter is considerably quieter, and casual conversation is possible between engineer and fireman. A control cab car also lacks the bone-rattling vibrations of a diesel locomotive cab—which experienced old timers say is itself nothing compared to its counterpart aboard a steam engine! On hot summer days, engine crews appreciate the fact their station at the end of the gallery deck enables them to enjoy the air conditioning. But many crew members like to hear and feel the diesel engine they're controlling and, from a technical point of view, when operating from the control cab the engineer can not make use of the separate engine brake, only the train brake. Control cab cars do have a special brake that can be used to hold a train at a station while the train brakes are released, but not a full engine brake as on a locomotive.[15]

Burlington, North Western, the Milwaukee Road, and even cash-poor Rock Island to a limited extent, managed to renew all or part of their commuter fleets with private capital. In 1964 Federal grants became available for capital investment in urban mass transit (a definition which includes suburban railroad service) and a fresh wave of fleet replacement began. But the railroads were still profit-seeking private corporations and the Federal legislation establishing the mass transit program specified that such grants go only to public agencies. What happened in several sub-regions of metropolitan Chicago, following the passage of permissive state legislation, was the creation of small, special-purpose public boards that fully qualified to be legal recipients of Federal assistance, and which then turned around and leased cars and locomotives to the various railroads. The Milwaukee Road was able to purchase more push-pull gallery cars and new locomotives. Burlington was able to re-build its original roster to full HEP configuration (i.e., eliminate the steam heat), and to buy more cars as well as a fleet of rebuilt E8 and E9 locomotives for use exclusively in suburban service. Also, under this dispensation, the region's most distinctive commuter service, provided by the Illinois Central RR, became even more so.

The uniqueness of the IC operation must be emphasized. It is the only commuter service in America that enjoys a right-of-way totally separate from the company's intercity lines, both freight and passenger, a practice quite common in Europe. Also, when electrification was installed in 1926 the rolling stock was the only suburban railroad equipment in America that utilized high-level platforms exclusively—no ground-level loading. The IC right-of-way is also different from other Chicago roads in that it hugs the shoreline of Lake Michigan before terminating near the Loop at Michigan and Randolph. Indeed, this proximity to the lake front generated public pressure in the 1920s to relocate the IC tracks so that the citizenry of Chicago would have better access to the water. The project thus became two-fold: relocate the tracks and electrify the suburban service.

In 1968, the Chicago South Suburban Mass Transit District, one of the local agencies formed as a conduit for Federal funds, ordered 130 new electric multiple-unit cars from the St. Louis Car Company to replace most, but not all, of IC's 1926-era stock. The design was in general imitation of the standard diesel-hauled gallery car, except it was self-powered, and so

HERE SHE COMES! Running left-hand, in the British tradition, a train of Chicago & North Western commuters thunders along the iron, bound for Crystal Lake, Illinois. Location: Des Plaines, Illinois.

incorporated a number of design modifications, among them a motorman's cab located in a vestibule at one end of each car, plus the permanent coupling of every two cars into a "married pair" set. In 1978, the local agency obtained an additional thirty-six units to phase out the remaining older cars. Low bidder on this contract was the Bombardier Company, of Quebec.

A date of consequence to Chicago transit in particular, and suburban railroad service in general, was March 19, 1974. That was the day voters in the six-county metropolitan area gave their approval to the creation of an all-embracing regional agency to oversee mass transportation in and around Chicago. Known as the RTA, for Regional Transportation Authority, the agency has managed to keep alive the Chicago tradition of controversy and acrimony over transit matters, but has also registered some solid accomplishments, between rounds, so to speak.

One of the new agency's first items of business was to purchase a fleet of fifty brand-new diesel locomotives from the Electro-Motive Division of General Motors. (EMD's manufacturing facility is conveniently at hand in suburban Chicago, the geographical location designated as McCook, Illinois.) A fleet of 124 new gallery cars were turned out by the Budd Company, expediting the complete conversion of Rock Island's commuter

THERE SHE GOES! Outbound C&NW commuter train rumbles over the diamond under the eye of the operator in Deval Tower, Des Plaines, watchdog of commuter traffic on C&NW's busy Northwest line where it crosses the Soo Line. Outsize floor-to-ceiling dimension of a gallery car is dramatically emphasized in this back-lighted hind-end view. (James M. Cudahy photo)

The new m.u. gallery cars that now provide all service on electrified lines of ICG have an impressive assortment of hardware on the business end: horn, bell, headlight, marker lights, number boards.

Left: IC memory. Before new bilevel m.u. cars were built for service on what is now called the Illinois Central Gulf RR, this is the style and shape of car that handled suburban service on Chicago's only electrified railroad.

services to full gallery-car, push-pull operation. The new equipment also permitted the re-equipping of a few oddball services: a lone Norfolk & Western train between Chicago and Orland Park over ex-Wabash trackage, as well as a single daily round trip between Chicago and Joliet over the former Gulf, Mobile & Ohio route. The GM&O merged with the Illinois Central in 1972 to form the Illinois Central Gulf. But the "Joliet Plug," as this train was affectionately called, continued to use equipment decorated in GM&O colors, including the last F-3 type diesel locomotive to haul passengers in regular service anyplace on the face of the earth. Not only did the RTA equip the existing trains on these one-round-trip-a-day routes with new rolling stock, it increased service by adding a second train.

RTA's design and graphics staff developed a spiffy blue, orange and brown livery for its fleet of new EMD F40PH diesels. After negotiations were completed to purchase outright all C&NW's commuter equipment, the new colors started to appear on that line's older cars and locomotives. One little glitch: RTA people had specified a type face called "Double Cable Bold" for all lettering and numerals. But when the C&NW began repainting some of the older diesels in the new scheme—C&NW crews performed this work under contract to the RTA—they went out and ordered

A two-car train of gallery m.u. cars zips along Illinois Central Gulf's four-track electrified line that hugs the shoreline of Lake Michigan south of downtown Chicago.

traditional "railroad gothic" numerals for the engines, thus mildly frustrating the RTA's efforts to speedily establish a modern corporate identity.

RTA and the railroads worked out arrangements whereby the public agency subsidizes the companies for operating suburban service. The companies are even able to earn incentive payments (i.e., profits, by whatever name) for superior performance. The negotiations preliminary to these arrangements were protracted and oft-times heated, but serious people were talking about serious issues—not to mention big dollars. The end result was the successful transformation of the region's commuter services into a publicly subsidized operation, although in a different pattern from three decades previously. Then it was the region's rapid transit system, and resulted in complete public takeover of the once-private corporations, whereas now the private railroad companies continue to manage and run the subsidized commuter services. Engineers and conductors remain company employees; they are not civil servants, although the equipment they operate belongs to the body politic.

CHAPTER NINETEEN
The Railroad Stations

Today's commuter fleets operate out of several terminals scattered around downtown Chicago on the edge of the Loop, if not actually in it. Time was when Chicago boasted many more, of course, and depots such as Dearborn Station, Grand Central Terminal and Central Station are no longer in business. But there are still four sizeable operating passenger train terminals, each of which has a distinctive character and heritage, and retains a measure of the bustling activity associated with the Great Days of railroad travel.[16]

Union Station presents the greatest variety. Here are five different commuter services plus all of Amtrak's intercity traffic. Union is unique, a terminal that is really two stub-end depots laid out back-to-back on either side of a central concourse.[17] Burlington-Northern, Norfolk & Western, and the ex-GM&O service to Joliet operate from the south side of the facility, as does the sole Chicago commuter service that falls outside the RTA's jurisdiction—a pair of daily round trips to Valparaiso, Indiana, over the old Pennsylvania Railroad.[18] These make no stops at all in the state of Illinois, other than Union Station. From PRR the service passed over to Penn Central, then to Conrail. Finally, thanks to a rescue effort launched by the United States Congress, the "Valpo locals" were assigned to Amtrak, despite an apparently conflicting statutory directive which prohibits that agency from operating service totally commuter in character. The equipment used on these trains by Amtrak is of interest and makes the two trains rather resemble typical Chicago commuter service. The cars are ex-Chicago & North Western gallery coaches bought by the C&NW in the 1950s for use on its intercity trains to places like Milwaukee and Green Bay. After it was created in 1971 Amtrak purchased this small fleet and put it to work for a spell on several of its services out of Chicago. Once Amtrak's own new equipment was delivered, the cars became surplus, and RTA even leased them from Amtrak to serve some time on the Rock Island. They proved to be the perfect fit for Amtrak's new commuter responsibilities in 1980 when Congress stepped in and saved the Valpo locals.

Across the concourse from all this activity is Union Station's considerably less busy north side, from which the Milwaukee Road provides commuter service over two lines, one due west to Elgin, the other north and then northwest to Fox Lake. From here a single round trip continues on, *sans* RTA subsidy, to serve Walworth, Wisconsin.[19]

Chicago & North Western has its own terminal a few blocks north of

Union Station and around the corner from the Chicago Civic Opera House—yet another legacy left to the city by a man named Insull. C&NW depot is an American big-city, big-railroad passenger terminal in the classic mold. Which, unfortunately, is also to say that it sits on a very valuable piece of downtown real estate the railroad wants to translate into income-producing property. Trains will continue to operate at the location, but the station seems likely to become an early casualty to development.

Today, C&NW depot is used exclusively by commuter trains. At one time the railroad, in joint operation with both the Union Pacific and the Southern Pacific, handled such trains as *The San Francisco Overland* and *The City of Los Angeles*, so that the Clinton and Madison depot was a major gateway to the west. In the early 1950s the California trains were rerouted over the Milwaukee Road (east of Omaha) but C&NW itself continued a reasonable schedule of intercity trains to points on its own lines in the upper Midwest. Its purchase of gallery cars for these services was one of the last investments in intercity equipment made by any American railroad, for instance. But with the creation of Amtrak in 1971, the line's passenger services beyond the commuter zone came to an end. Also removed from C&NW depot by virtue of Amtrak's creation were a couple of trains operated by the B&O and the C&O. These had moved into the C&NW facility several months earlier when B&O's own Chicago terminal, Grand Central, was closed.[20]

Rock Island continues to use La Salle Street Station, and up until 1981, one could say this was at least one Chicago railroad terminal that was truly handy to a CRT/CTA Loop L station. Before 1981, it was possible to walk directly from the L station to the concourse of the railroad terminal without descending to street level. But no longer. At one time, RTA gave serious thought to moving the entire Rock Island service out of La Salle Street altogether and transferring all operations to Union Station. But an alternative plan won out. The bumping posts have been moved 350 feet to the south to allow the old terminal building that fronts on Van Buren Street to be given over to developers for new commercial construction. A small terminal has been erected at the new site, a block south of the older one.[21]

The Rock Island, incidently, while it no longer exists as a common carrier railroad, was one of three American railroads that continued to operate intercity passenger trains after the creation of Amtrak.[22] *The Peoria Rocket*, between Chicago and Peoria, and *The Quad City Rocket*, between Chicago and Rock Island (a municipality often lumped with Moline, East Moline and Davenport and referred to as "Quad Cities"), left Chicago each evening and returned the next morning, similar to the service pattern of a commuter operation. But the pair catered not to daily workers enroute to jobs in downtown Chicago, rather to business people with appointments and shoppers heading for a day at Marshall Field's. Absolute statements about transportation matters are always risky, but these two Rock Island trains—before they received the benefit of public subsidies from the state of Illinois in the fall of 1971—were the last fully privately operated intercity passenger trains to serve Chicago. They were abandoned outright on the last day of 1978, although the state and Amtrak got together to institute a substitute Peoria-Chicago service over the ICG and the Toledo, Peoria & Western. It proved short lived, however, and has since been abandoned.

The Illinois Central is more properly, but not always, called the Illinois Central Gulf since its merger with the Gulf, Mobile & Ohio. But it is the only Chicago railroad that can boast more than one downtown passenger station. Its terminal is at (and under) Randolph Street, just east of Michigan Avenue[23], but inbound and outbound trains stop at Van Buren Street, eight-tenths of a mile south, and also at Roosevelt Road, still further south. Adjacent to the electric line's station here is a large tract of land that was, once upon a time Central Station, where IC's fleet of intercity trains terminated. This facility was built for the opening of the World's Columbian Exposition in 1893 and replaced an earlier IC station at South Water Street called Great Central Depot, opened in 1856. Great Central stood virtually on the same site as does IC's Randolph Street station today. An earlier edifice that occupied some of the real estate was Old Fort Dearborn, a Federal stockade built in 1803 and which, in 1812, became the scene of an historic massacre.

When Central Station opened in 1893, IC suburban trains continued to operate to South Water Street. Central Station itself survived into the Amtrak era, but not for long. In early 1972 Amtrak rerouted all its intercity services into Union Station and the grand old IC terminal was torn down.

And thus completes the story of how commuter railroad service in Chicago passed from the domain of unbridled private enterprise to the shaky sanctuary of a publicly subsidized activity. But as a concluding note on the matter of subsidized commuter service, let us hark back to an earlier time. In the early 1850s the Illinois Central Railroad was buying up land, laying track, and in general participating to the full in the pell-mell race to crisscross the Middle West with railroads. But standing astride the line's proposed right-of-way into the heart of Chicago was a 300-acre parcel of undeveloped land owned by a gentleman named Paul Cornell. Today this territory is called Hyde Park and few who know the area could possibly imagine it was once wilderness. Mr. Cornell and the railroad tried to come to terms, but couldn't until, finally, the following suggestion was advanced.

In exchange for selling the railroad a right-of-way through his land, the Illinois Central would agree to operate a short-haul passenger train between downtown Chicago and Mr. Cornell's undeveloped—but soon to be developed—tract. And so it happened that on July 21, 1856, the first train so operated, *with nary a passenger aboard*. But Cornell was not unreasonable, and his agreement with the IC carried this stipulation: should the suburban passenger service not return sufficient revenue to the railroad, why then he, Paul Cornell, would make up the shortfall with a direct subsidy. Indeed, during the difficult days brought on by the Panic of 1857 this is exactly what happened.

The RTA may have felt it was plowing new ground when it began large scale subsidization of commuter railroad service in 1975. But please don't tell Paul Cornell about it.

Notes to Part Three

[1]An order for 500 cars, to be built by the Kilbourne and Jacobs Mfg. Co., of Columbus, Ohio, had these specifications: length, twelve feet, six inches; width, three feet, nine inches; weight, empty, 3,610 pounds; capacity, 15,000 pounds. Trucks featured fourteen-inch wheels and cast steel side frames, automatic knuckle couplers and draft gear, but no train brakes—all braking being supplied by the locomotive.

[2]See: George W. Hilton and John F. Due, *The Electric Interurban Railways in America* (Stanford, California: Stanford University Press, 1960 and 1964); William D. Middleton, *The Interurban Era* (Milwaukee, Wisconsin: Kalmbach Publishing Company, 1961).

[3]See: *The Great Third Rail* (Chicago: Central Electric Railfans Association, 1961 and 1970).

[4]See: William D. Middleton, *North Shore* (San Marino, California: Golden West Books, 1964); *Interurban to Milwaukee* (Chicago: Central Electric Railfans Association, 1962 and 1974); *Route of the Electroliners* (Chicago: Central Electric Railfans Association, 1963 and 1975). Of the last two volumes, the first covers until 1926, the second afterward.

[5]See: William D. Middleton, *South Shore* (San Marino, California: Golden West Books, 1970).

[6]Even before the IC electrification was installed in 1926, South Shore cars, but not entire trains, were hauled into downtown Chicago behind IC steam engines. The first through South Shore electric train operated into downtown Chicago on August 29, 1926, three weeks after the railroad's electrification was inaugurated.

[7]For an interesting account of the South Shore's survival, see: George M. Smerk, "South Shore Renaissance," *Indiana Business Review* (February, 1980), pp. 2–9.

[8]Early in 1982, the first new m.u. car to be built for the South Shore since the Insull days arrived on the property. Turned out by Nippon-Sharyo of Japan, it was the first unit of a 36-car order purchased for the railroad by the Northern Indiana Commuter Transportation District (NICTD). Price tag for the new cars was 49 million dollars, including a supply of spare parts.

[9]After World War II the line was reorganized and became the Chicago, Aurora & Elgin *Railway*.

Diesel celebrity. Before the RTA replaced the Rock Island's aging motive power with spanking new EMD F40PH diesels, one of the units powering the Rock's commuter trains was No. 630, the last active E6 type passenger unit in service in the country. The graceful slanting nose of the E6 dates this locomotive to the streamlining era of the early 1940s. The 630 posed for this picture at Blue Island, Illinois, in March, 1975.

[10]One can ride a lovingly restored CA&E car in places as far away as Maine and Connecticut. But in South Elgin, Illinois, on the ground of the R.E.L.I.C. Museum, several cars still run on a piece of trackage that was once part of the local Fox River Valley trolley system, a corporate kin of the "Roaring Elgin." Former North Shore cars operate at several trolley museums, and at the Illinois Railway Museum in Union, a collection of ex-CRT L cars can be found.

[11]For further details see: Thomas Buck, *Skokie Swift* (Chicago: Chicago Transit Authority, 1968).

[12]See: Alan A. Jackson, *London's Termini* (New York: Augustis M. Kelley, 1969).

[13]See, for example: John F. Stover, *History of the Illinois Central Railroad* (New York: Macmillan, 1975); Richard C. Overton, *Burlington Route* (New York: Knopf, 1965).

[14]For a discussion of C&NW's approach to its commuter services during this period by a man who would later become president of the railroad, see: Larry S. Provo, "Chicago and North Western Railway Company's Program for Modernization of Its Suburban Operation," *Proceedings of the Annual Conference on Taxation*, ed. Walter J. Kress (Harrisburg, Pennsylvania: National Tax Association, 1961), pp. 242–248.

[15]Most roads permit smoking in certain gallery cars, with the control cab car being a convenient one so to designate. C&NW engine crews objected, and now the passenger compartment where the engine crews work is a non-smoker.

Parmelee motor omnibuses of the 1920s.

[16]During the heyday of intercity railroad passenger service, downtown Chicago boasted yet another distinctive passenger transport system, the Parmelee Transportation Company. Begun in 1853 by a young man from Genesee County in New York by the name of Frank Parmelee, the company specialized in transferring passengers and their luggage from one Chicago rail depot to another, or to a downtown hotel. By 1881, Parmelee operated seventy-five passenger coaches, seventy-five baggage wagons, and 250 horses. Parmelee himself sold the company in 1903 (and he died in 1904), but the enterprise continued to grow even when motor vehicles replaced the original horse-drawn fleet. The Parmelee Company's railroad station transfer service was phased out in the 1950s, but today's Continental Air Transport Company, whose buses carry passengers between the Loop and Chicago's two airports, is a corporate descendant of Parmelee.

[17]One or two tracks run "through" Union Station at the east end, and at one time Amtrak actually operated Milwaukee-St. Louis service with Chicago as a mere intermediate stop using these tracks. RTA has toyed with the idea of making major alterations to Union Station and operating similar run-through commuter service.

[18]RTA determined it would only subsidize commuter service when the entire trip was within the state of Illinois. A 1976 survey turned up the fact that 18 percent of the riders on the South Shore travel totally within Illinois; hence RTA

Heading for Michigan City, Indiana, an afternoon train on the Chicago, South Shore & South Bend makes its final stop along the ICG line. Ahead, it will swing onto its own iron, the nation's last true interurban railway. . . .

subsidizes the old Insull line to that extent. This policy also caused the C&NW to cut the Lake Geneva, Wisconsin, branch back to short of the Wisconsin state line. C&NW's north line continues to terminate in Kenosha, Wisconsin, however because this station provides the only proper turn-around facilities for trains that serve Winthrop Harbor and Zion, Illinois.

[19]The current Union Station was opened in 1925, replacing an earlier 1880-built facility on the same site. There are fourteen tracks on the south side and ten on the north. Originally there were two major buildings in the Union Station complex: a waiting room on the west side of Clinton Street and a concourse providing access to platforms on the east side, connected by underground passageways. In the early 1970s the building over the train concourse was torn down and replaced by a high-rise office building. The waiting room still stands.

[20]One of C&NW's corporate predecessors, the Galena and Chicago Union, began service into the city's very first passenger terminal in 1848. It was located at Canal and Kinzie, just north of the current terminal. In 1880 the company opened its second terminal, at Wells and Kinzie, today the site of the Merchandise Mart. A problem with this site was that the Chicago River drawbridge, which trains had to use entering and leaving the terminal, was forever being raised and lowered for river traffic, thereby disrupting train schedules.

The current terminal opened in 1911. Tracks approach the terminal at second story level on an embankment, and the depot was originally built with sixteen passenger tracks, one of which has since been eliminated to permit construction of a walkway to the CTA's Lake Street L. C&NW Depot features a Bush train shed, a style of facility designed by Lincoln Bush of the Delaware, Lackawanna & Western Railroad and first installed at that company's Hoboken Terminal.

[21]The Michigan Southern & Rock Island Depot was built on the site of La Salle Street Station in 1871 and suffered serious damage in the famous Chicago fire of that same year. It was rebuilt in 1872. The recently abandoned La Salle Street Station opened in 1903 and included eleven passenger tracks, all at second-story level.

[22]Unable to work its way out of receivership, the Chicago, Rock Island & Pacific Railroad was liquidated in early 1980. Other midwest railroads took over key freight routes and the RTA gained control of the forty-mile Chicago–Joliet main line, plus a seven-mile branch line. RTA continues to operate the suburban service, which commuters still call the "Rock Island."

[23]Illinois Central Gulf's Randolph Street Station is a below-ground facility that was built as part of the electrification and track realignment program in 1926. Originally there were six tracks; today, but five are used for passenger alighting and boarding.

Postscripts

TO CHAPTER FOURTEEN: END OF THE LOOP?

I

"The Union Loop, a massive web of riveted steel girders and shining tracks, arches over busy city streets, passing close by the windows of tall buildings on either side, and insistently threads its way through downtown Chicago. . . .

"For the industrial archeologist, the Chicago Loop provides an *ideal case study of an entire transit system of reasonably manageable size that still serves its original purpose.* The elevated structures and commuter stations still remain in relatively good condition. The stations, like the one at Quincy Street (see next page), are excellent examples of metallic architecture in the exuberant classical style made fashionable by Chicago's World's Columbian Exposition in 1893."

—from INDUSTRIAL ARCHEOLOGY: A New Look at the American Heritage, by Theodore Anton Sande (1976, The Stephen Greene Press). The author is a director of the National Trust for Historic Preservation, and the "founding father" (in 1972) and first president of the Society for Industrial Archeology.

(*Continued next page*)

Left: Van Buren and Dearborn Streets (Jack E. Boucher)

Above: Randolph Street at Wabash Avenue (Jack E. Boucher)

Station, Quincy Street at Wells Street. (This and the two preceding photos are by Jack E. Boucher, reproduced courtesy of the Historic American Engineering Record, National Park Service)

"Industrial archeology" is a new field of study, extending the "national monument" concept to industry: the discovery, investigation, recording, surveying, and sometimes the preservation of historically significant industrial sites and structures. The Chicago Loop is in the category of transportation, as industry, which includes such "artifacts" as bridges, viaducts, railroad stations, ferry buildings, etc. In the quoted excerpt, the italics are ours.

II

"With respect to its historic significance, the Department of Interior noted in the determination of eligibility for the National Register (July 1978) that the Loop El is important both as an historic transportation facility as well as for its influence on the growth and development of downtown Chicago. The Loop El is also significant as an example of riveted steel elevated transit construction.

". . . the proposed improvements will serve to ensure that the El continues to perform those functions in a safer, more responsive way."

—from a Memorandum re the Proposed Loop El Rehabilitation Project, U.S. Department of Transportation, Urban Mass Transportation Administration, April 12, 1982.

Appendices

A contemporary view of Lake and Wells, looking toward the southeast. Four-car train of 6000 series cars is an Evanston Express that has finished its circuit of the Loop. It will continue straight ahead, cross the tracks of the Lake-Dan Ryan line, and head back to the Wilmette terminal over the former Northwestern L (CTA photo)

APPENDIX 1: CTA Rapid Transit Service to Chicago and Suburb

This schematic diagram clearly locates the A and B stops for trains so designated by these letters. It is a portion of the superb CTA bus/subway/L route map issued in 1975 (to which we've added the lake shore as orientation for out-of-towners).

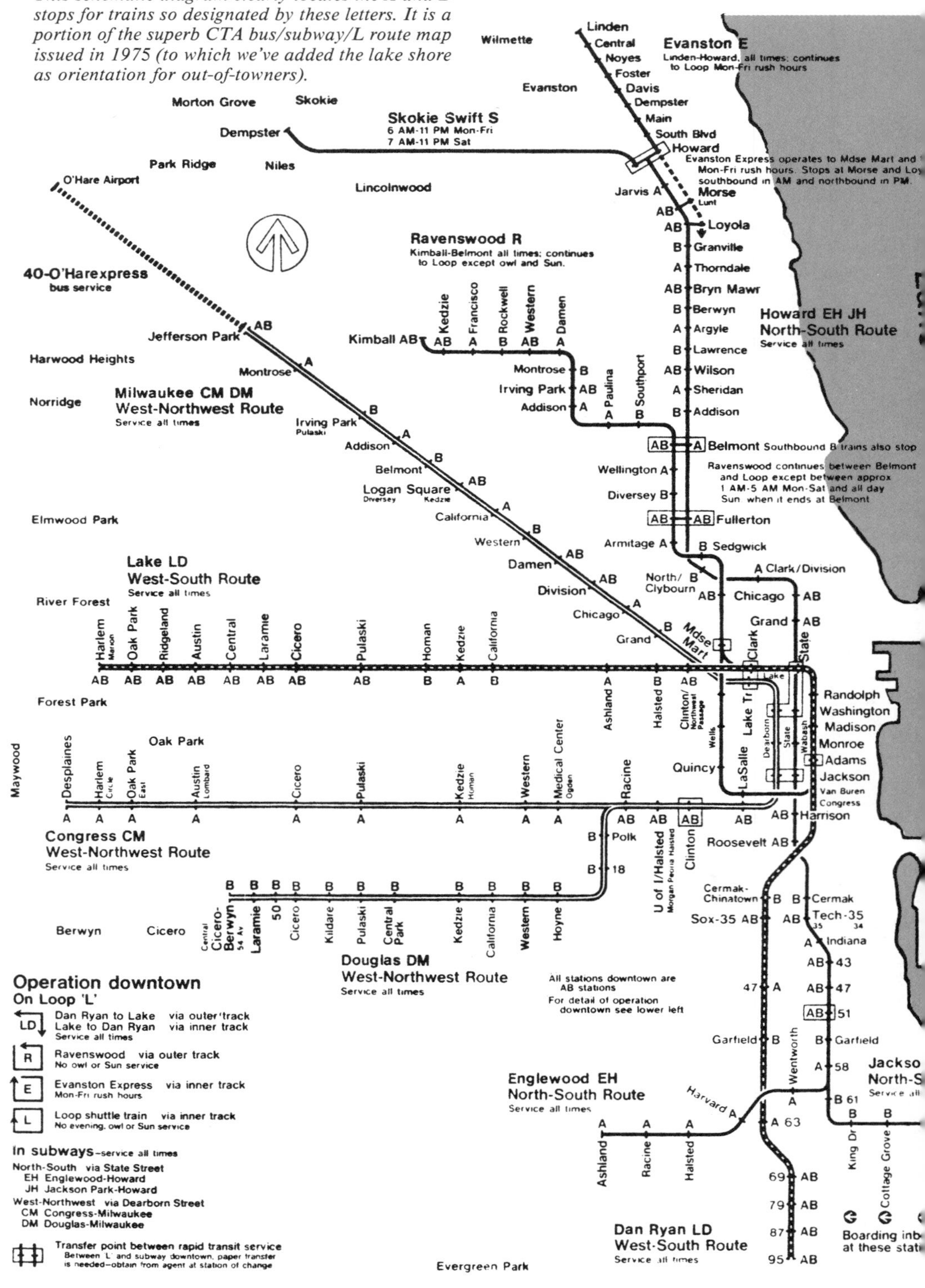

APPENDIX 2: CTA Rapid Transit System; Revenue Passenger Equipment

Numbers	*Builder*	*Date*	*Motors*	*Weight*	*Style*	*Notes*
5-50	St. Louis Car	1959-'60	4 @ 55 hp	47,000	single units	(1)
51-52	Pullman	1947	8 @ 55 hp	94,800	3 section articulated	(2)
53-54	St. Louis Car	1948	8 @ 55 hp	92,700	3 section articulated	(2)
2001-2180	Pullman	1964	4 @ 100 hp	47,300	married pair	(3)
2201-2350	Budd	1969-'70	4 @ 100 hp	45,000	" " "	(3)
2401-2600	Boeing-Vertol	1976-'78	4 @ 110 hp	50,500	" " "	(3) (5)
2601-3200	Budd	1981-'84	4 @ 110 hp	54,300	" " "	(3) (5)
4271-4272	Cincinnati	1923	2 @ 160 hp	76,800	single units	(5)
6001-6720	St. Louis Car	1950-'59	4 @ 55 hp	42,000	married pair	(4)

Notes

(1) Cars 1 through 4 retired
(2) Experimental cars from post-war era; retained for Skokie Swift service
(3) Air-conditioned
(4) Series will be systematically retired as 2600 series Budd cars are delivered; many converted to non-revenue uses; some units will likely be retained for emergency use.
(5) Equipped with conventional transit sliding doors; all other CTA cars eqipped with "trolley-car style" folding (or "blinker") doors.

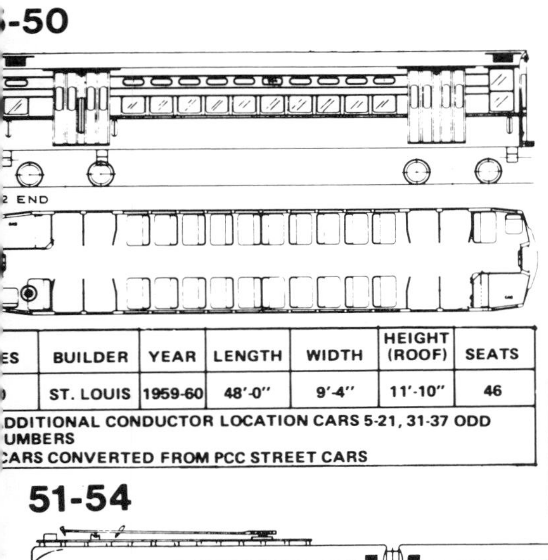

ES	BUILDER	YEAR	LENGTH	WIDTH	HEIGHT (ROOF)	SEATS
)	ST. LOUIS	1959-60	48'-0"	9'-4"	11'-10"	46

DDITIONAL CONDUCTOR LOCATION CARS 5-21, 31-37 ODD
UMBERS
CARS CONVERTED FROM PCC STREET CARS

Rail system

Passenger cars in service*

11-1-80 jwh

Drawings and specifications here, on following pages, and of the 6000 series (page 90) are courtesy of CTA, General Operations Division. (Author's collection)

*Assignment as of Nov. 1, 1980

SERIES	BUILDER	YEAR	LENGTH	WIDTH	HEIGHT (ROOF)	SEATS
51-52 53-54	PULLMAN ST. LOUIS	1947 1948	88'-7½"	9'-4"	12'-2"	96
EACH THREE COMPARTMENT CAR HAS ONE NUMBER						

51-54

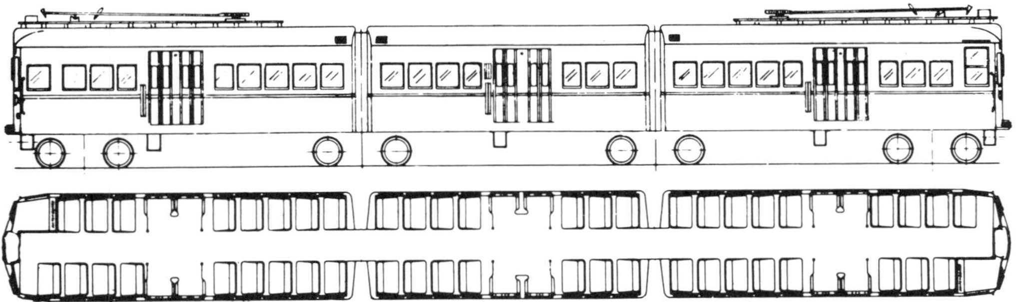

APPENDIX 2 (continued)

2001-2180

2201-2350

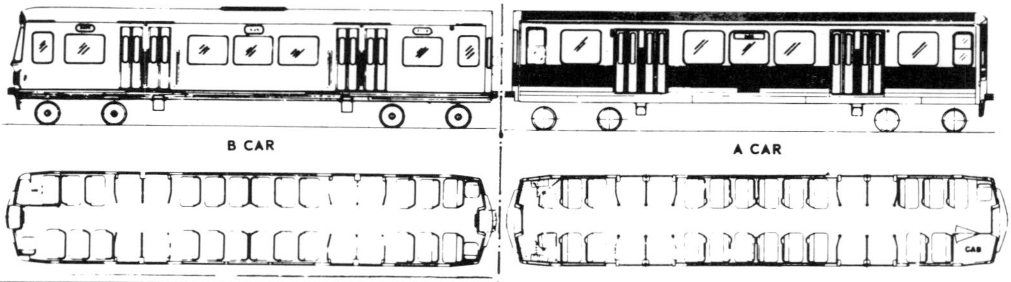

B CAR

A CAR

SERIES	BUILDER	YEAR	LENGTH	WIDTH	HEIGHT (ROOF)	SEATS
2001-2180 2201-2350	PULLMAN BUDD	1964 1969-70	48′-0″	9′-4″	12′-0″	A-47,B-51

DIAGRAMS ARE COMBINED TO SAVE SPACE; CARS ARE PERMANENTLY COUPLED IN CONSECUTIVELY NUMBERED PAIRS STARTING WITH 2001-2002

SERIES	BUILDER	YEAR	LENGTH	WIDTH	HEIGHT (ROOF)	SE
2401-2600	BOEING-VERTOL	1976-1978	48′-0″	9′-4″	12′-0″	A- B-

2401-2600

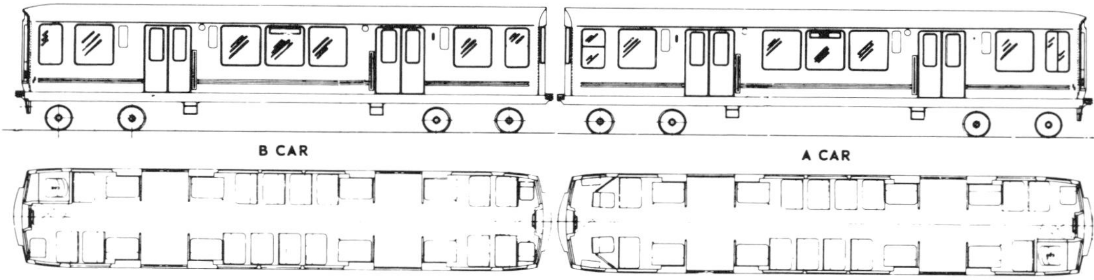

B CAR

A CAR

2601–2602

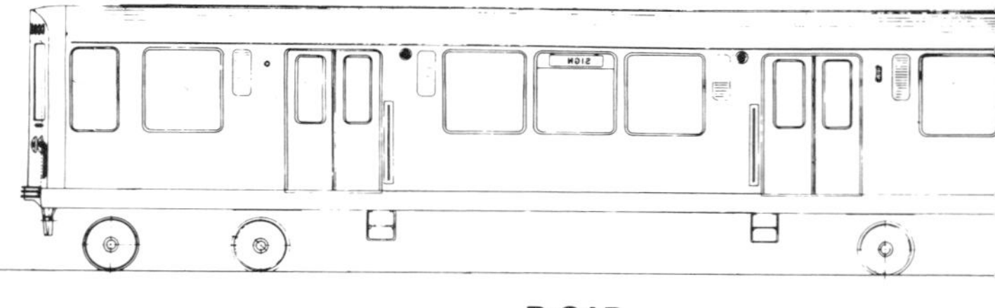

B CAR

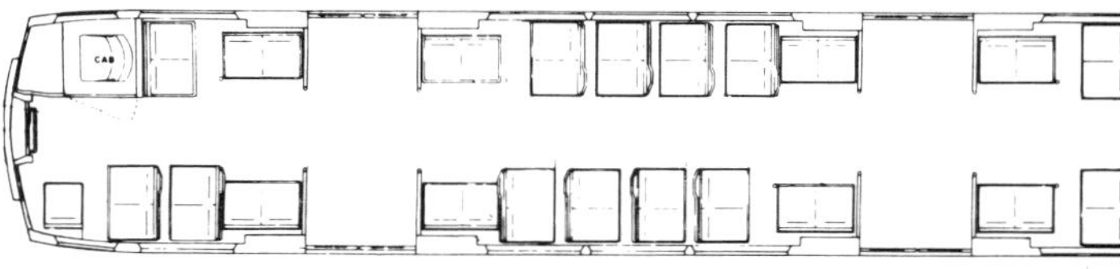

Above: First Units in car series 2601–2900, by Budd

Left: End view of car No. 2602 (CTA photo)

4271-4272

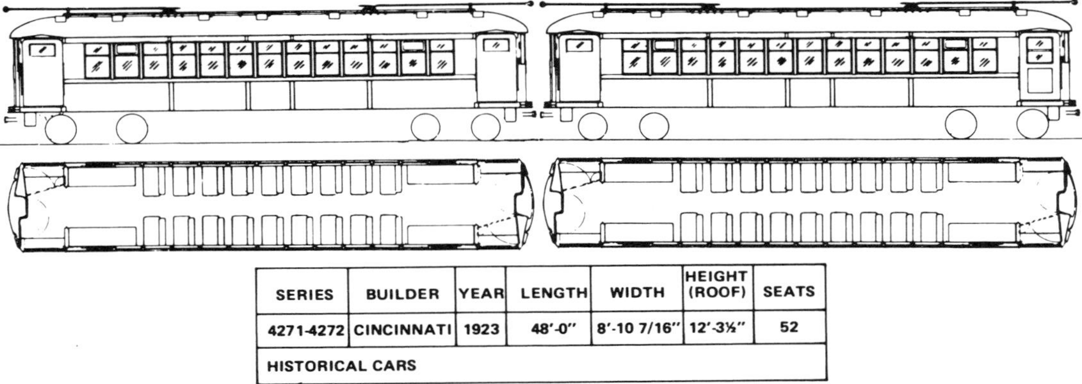

SERIES	BUILDER	YEAR	LENGTH	WIDTH	HEIGHT (ROOF)	SEATS
4271-4272	CINCINNATI	1923	48'-0"	8'-10 7/16"	12'-3½"	52
HISTORICAL CARS						

OVER THE YEARS, conservatism and sharp curves have kept the Chicago Transit Authority from veering toward radical redesign of its rapid transit cars. Thus, CTA today operates five generations of 48-foot cars that at first glance seem quite conventional. In this case, however, first glances can be deceiving.

Like their predecessors, the new Budd cars are short enough to negotiate the 89-foot radius curves in elevated segments of the CTA rail system. But at 54,300 pounds, they're the heaviest of the fleet. Their weight includes trucks that CTA claims are the best ever, for smooth sailing at top speed of 70 mph and maximum acceleration of 3.2 mph per second.

The Wegmann-built trucks have flexible frames and primary springs, and are mounted totally in rubber. They have no air springs, ball joints, equalizing bars, sliding or contracting surfaces. A wheel can rise more than two inches without affecting other wheels.

The cars run on three-phase, 230-volt, 60Hz alternating current, which improves reliability and reduces costs.

The first 100 are [in] service on the West/Northwest line . . . When all 600 are delivered, CTA will have a fleet of 1,120 "universal" cars.

—Excerpts from "CTA Cars: No Frills, No Nonsense" by Frank Malone. RAILWAY AGE, May 10, 1982

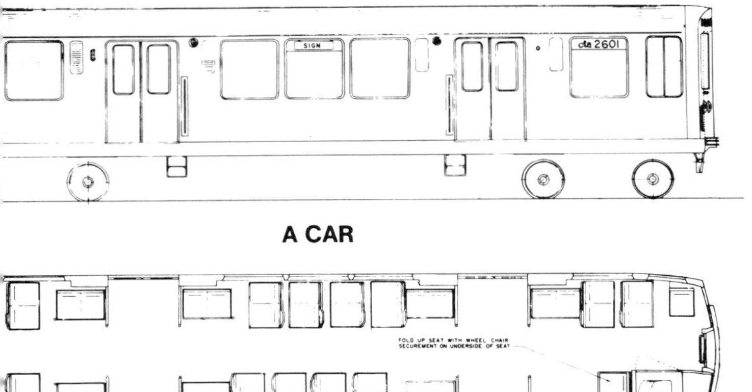

SPECIFICATIONS:

Length, 48 feet
Height, 12 feet
Width, 8 ft. 8 in. (platform)
9 ft. 4 in. (window sill)
Weight, 54,300 pounds
Seats, 92 per pair
Construction, Stainless Steel
Propulsion, electric, 110 hp traction motors
Balance speed, 70 mph
Max. acceleration, 3.2 mphps
Max. service brake, 3.2 mphps

The 2600s operate as "married pairs." Specifications from CTA

APPENDIX 3: Chicago-area Commuter Railroad Service (as of Jan. 1, 1981)

Railroad	*Route Miles*	*Stations*	*Trains/ Weekday*	*Cars*	*Locomotives*
Burlington Northern	38	26	64	141	25
Chicago & North Western	165	50	200	280	76
Milwaukee Road	110	44	73	132	23
Rock Island	47	28	60	89	18
Norfolk & Western	16	15	4	16	2
Illinois Central Gulf (ex-GM&O route)	33	9	4	8	2
Illinois Central Gulf (ex-IC routes)	39	50	230	165	(1)
Chicago, South 90 Shore & South Bend	90	36	39	54	(1,2)

Notes
(1) Electric powered multiple unit cars
(2) All other passenger cars shown are air conditioned gallery car-type vehicles; South Shore fleet dates to the 1920s, is entirely single level, and all units are not air conditioned. First car of a car order of new equipment to replace all or most of these older cars arrived in January, 1982.

At right: Angular and functional is a good description of the new F40PH General Motors diesel locomotives built for Chicago suburban service in the RTA era. Similar locomotives haul commuters in Toronto, Boston and northern New Jersey. The same locomotive has also become the work horse of the Amtrak roster.

Below and opposite page: Diagonal head-end bars, and stripe between windows, of the ICG m.u. gallery cars are bright red, accenting the overall black and steely gray decor. (RTA graphic, author's collection)

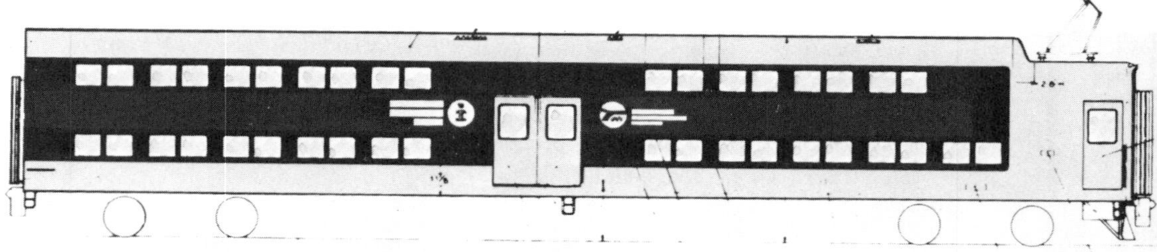

Two Boeing-Vertol cars, with Chicago's towering skyline in the background, head for the Dan Ryan line south of the downtown area. (CTA)

INDEX

Wabash Avenue leg on the Union looking north, circa 1974.